The Pangram Killer

Brandon M. Lipani

ISBN: 151954037X
ISBN-13: 978-1519540379

DEDICATION

This book is dedicated to my wife, daughter, mother and father for always supporting me in everything I do in my life. I would be lost without the four of you.

CONTENTS

ACKNOWLEDGMENTS

I would like to thank everyone who helped me with this book I could not have done it without you.

Prologue

Andy and his partner Jeff pull up to the warehouse in their department issued crown Vic. The two men are the detectives on call tonight. Andy gets out, seeing them putting a young cop in his early 20's into a body bag.

Andy is upset by this. The guy probably just got out of the academy a few years ago and now he is dead. "What a waste", he thought to himself. Andy looks around and he thinks to himself "Someone had to be brave to knock over a police warehouse".

Andy walks over to one of the warehouse doors. There were bullet holes. He knew semi-automatic weapons and, judging from the ammo shells, these were rec7, which is usually department issued to swat teams.

Andy had heard over the radio they had one guy on his way to hospital with a wound and two guys got away. He knew by looking at the scene this was going to be headline news tomorrow in the paper and on TV news tonight.

He looked over at his partner. He was gazing over things not taking this as serious as

Andy wanted but his partner only had two weeks left till he transferred out of homicide. Andy would be getting a new young partner, a woman named Serena Triton. She had passed her detective exam and was moving up. Andy was excited to get a new partner. He hoped to have this case solved by the time he started working with her in a few weeks.

CHAPTER 1

As the sun beads in through the window, Serena Triton sits at her table in her small New York apartment in the Bronx reading the newspaper and doing a crossword puzzle. Serena has made this her morning routine since starting her detective job about six months ago in the NYPD. When she was a cop on the beat, she liked reading the paper in the morning to see what arrests had taken place. She liked to see what her co-workers on other shifts were up to on a regular basis.

She also enjoyed the crossword puzzle the best. She would do the puzzle right after she had read the comics. The comics were something she had started reading as a little girl. Her father would give them to her every morning out of his paper and she would read them. This was kind of something that just followed her as a habit into her older years.

Serena was a 29 year old single woman who lived alone. She had long black hair about shoulder length, green eyes and a small build. Standing at about 5 foot 10 inches, she was a force to be reckoned with at the academy. She made up for her smaller build with her drive, enthusiasm and being sharp as a tack. She graduated top of her class in high school and could have gone to any college she wanted on a full scholarship. She chose to join the police academy as her pick. She used scholarship money to pay for her academy training and detective training. She graduated top of her class in academics and was in top 3 for physical training and marksmanship.

She was always physically fit in high school. She had a job working at a local gym after school a few nights a week and, while going to the academy, worked there as well. Running a few miles was nothing to her. She had a runner's build and enjoyed the fresh air and time to think. She felt it helped her clear her head for her studies.

Looking at the time, Serena knew she

had to get a move on getting to work on time. She only had half the crossword puzzle done. She was a little upset by that but knew she could finish it up when she got home from work. Serena was a bit of a game and puzzle nut. Her ideal night was some wine and a game, puzzle or book. Even as a child she had always been cursed with a mind that would never let her leave a puzzle undone or an answer unknown. This was kind of the reason she wanted to be a detective. Finding the answer to an unknown puzzle appealed to her.

As she goes to walk over to her living room table to get the items she needs for work, Serena glances over at her book shelf which consisted of mystery and murder novels. These books always inspired her to be a police officer. Never once did she ever think she would get her dream job as a detective. Serena notices a few good romance novels that she read and kept on her shelves. Serena was a hopeless romantic that had always dreamed of settling down with Mr. Right. Meeting him was hard. Most men were intimated by a female who was a homicide detective. But she was still young and had plenty of time to find the right man. Right now her main concern was her new job and being the best detective possible.

As she got ready for work, she clipped her badge and her gun on her belt then put her leather jacket on. It was still chilly out in the morning and she would rather be too warm than too cold. Plus it was easier for her to conceal her gun on the way into work. As she walked out and grabbed her keys and her cell phone, she noticed her small terrier, Muzzy, needed water. She quickly filled the water before running out being pressed for time.

As she gets down the stairs and into her car, she gives the wave to her neighbor Mrs. Magoogan. She was a sweet old lady maybe in her early 70's. She had a tough time getting around walking and doing daily tasks but she always managed to get outside and water her plants in the summer. Serena always admired that and hoped one day she could learn to have a nice, relaxing life after her time on the police force was over.

As she walks into the office carrying the coffee she had just picked up from the local coffee shop, she stops at her partner Andy's desk. She sits on the corner of his desk and puts his coffee down in front of him. Andy was quite a different type of man than Serena was used to. Andy was very well built and very strong with a domineering presence. He was of Italian descent which gave him kind of a tough guy edge. He kept his hair slicked back and very clean shaven as Andy always was presentable. His shirt was always pressed and his suits were always dry cleaned. A habit that Andy had picked up from his years in the military.

He was on his desk phone discussing with a fellow detective about a recent murder that had happened. Looking at his desk, Serena did not recognize the file or the case number. She was curious as to what this was regarding. While she was waiting for Andy to get off the phone, she noticed the updated picture of Andy's family. Andy had a wife of 10 years and two boys who were 7 and 9. Andy started dating his wife about a year after he graduated from the academy. That was another trait she had admired about Andy was his family orientation.

Serena had grown up in a single family environment. Her mom and dad divorced when she was a small girl. Her dad had raised her the best he could by himself. Her dad was a traffic cop for many years. Serena wanted to be a cop because of her dad but aspired to be more than just a traffic cop. She wanted what she felt was the big time homicide. She started at this precinct as a beat cop and worked her way to homicide. This took her several years and she was proud of her success and accomplishment. Andy was more experienced. He had been in this department almost 3 years and at the time was kind of mentoring Serena. She and Andy got along well so she did not mind it. She took his criticisms more as a friendly advice rather than a scolding.

When Andy hung up, Serena asked him what was going on and if she should review the file. Andy explained that there was a body found in the park this morning. It was of a man approximately in his mid 30's with his wallet and everything. Nothing had apparently been stolen from him. Andy also explained that they were being asked to investigate these murders by their boss. The two of them decided to head out to the park right away to investigate the scene.

As the two of them arrive at the scene, they speak with the first officer on the scene. He explained the man's body was found behind the park bench. Serena walks over to the bench after finishing her conversation with the black and white. She notices the man was face down with his overcoat on. She puts on her rubber gloves and notices a newspaper with red marker on the front page saying

"Zuriel's Yelling Could Not Stop The Quick Brown Fox From Jumping Over The Dog."

She starts searching the man to find his wallet on ground right next to him. From a quick look, she notices that all paperwork and money is untouched. This rules out a mugging or theft being a motive. Andy walks up behind her and notices the paper with the phrase. Andy makes a comment regarding the paper saying it's unusual. In the meantime, Serena opens the wallet and pulls the driver license out noticing the man's name was Zuriel.

Zuriel was an African American man. He was tall about 6 foot 2 inches and for the most part looked to be well built and in shape.

She shows the license to Andy. He glances at it and says "I know this guy. He worked at our precinct at one time in the cage cleaning weapons, checking out gear, stuff like

11

that. He left for a better position not too long ago." Andy calls over the forensics investigator Jessica that works with the homicide team.

Serena had not worked with Jessica too much in the 6 months she's been a detective. Jessica spent most of the time in the lab as of late considering she was 8 months pregnant. Going to crime scenes was a little tough on her. Normally, the detectives would just bring the evidence back to her. For this particular situation, Jessica wanted to actually see the scene since it was not a straightforward murder. Serena knew very little about Jessica. The only thing she really knew was she graduated from college top of her class then went to the academy. She graduated the academy with Andy. The two of them had become close friends between the time at the academy and working together for years. Serena had heard they had dated a little bit during the time at the academy. As it was something Andy told her in confidence, Serena always kept that information in the back of her mind.

Jessica walked over and started taking pictures of the scene as well as bagging up the newspaper with the letters in red marker.

Jessica explains she will take blood work to check for toxins, drugs or any other substances. Serena explains something is definitely weird. There were no signs of a struggle and nothing was stolen. Andy asks if Serena thinks it was suicide. She explains it's possible but why such a weird suicide letter? The two of them examine the scene closer then leave to head back to the office to examine the evidence.

Once back at the office, the two detectives examine the evidence. Serena keeps looking at the letter wondering what it means while Andy examines the pictures. Serena then asks Andy "How long it will be before the blood work is back?" Andy replies "It takes about 24 hours for that to come back." Serena explains she is going down to the lab to examine the body again for additional clues they may have missed.

As Serena get to the lab, she notices Jessica examining the body. Serena asks if she notices anything new. Jessica says "Besides the bruises on his stomach and thighs, he also has multiple prick marks on his fingers. But nothing that really stands out as foul play. I am sure the blood work will tell us more." Jessica explains that she is going to put a rush on the blood work. She has already drawn two vials and may need a few more. Jessica struggles to get on the lab stool and Serena asks if she is ok.

Jessica replies "Yeah, sometimes it tough getting around when you're this far along." Serena then asks "Are you and your boyfriend really excited?" Jessica then replies quickly and with a sarcastic tone "What boyfriend. I'm doing this by myself. Whatever doesn't kill you just makes you stronger. Right?"

Serena and Jessica laugh together and proceed to talk about the case. Jessica explains that there were no fingerprints on anything she checked. Everything, including the bench, clothing, newspaper and the wallet were clean. Not even the victim's fingerprints were on any of the items signifying this was definitely someone trying to cover their tracks.

Serena checks over the body looking at the obvious things but again notices nothing. Andy then opens the door to the lab and walks in walking around the body. Serena asks Andy if he is ok. Andy replies "Well not really. I have not been completely honest with you Serena. I know this man. We went to the academy together."

Serena then turns to Jessica and asks her if she remembers this victim. She shakes her head and explains that she knew a lot of people and does remember him from the academy. Andy explains that he remembers Zuriel speaking of a sister who lived down town. He explains that he would like to go see her and find out more information.

As Serena sits in the passenger seat of the unmarked police car she looks at Andy sitting in the driver seat. Andy had a complete look of focus and seriousness. Serena asks Andy why he withheld the information about knowing the victim. Andy explains that he was never this close to an investigation and was a bit shaken and it won't happen again.

As they pull up to the apartment complex, Serena checks the direction to see what apartment Zuriel's sister lived in so she could ring the bell. The complex was not in the greatest of areas but times were tough in the city and people were lucky to have a roof over their head at all. Serena and Andy walk up the stairs and Serena rings the bell. There is an answer on the other end. Andy explains they are detectives and need to speak with her regarding her brother. She invites them up to her 3rd floor apartment. Serena quickly asks what to call the women before they get up to the apartment. Andy says "Lenore. Her name is Lenore."

As they climb the stairs, the building gave off an old, eerie feeling. You could tell the building was not maintained which was typical of the landlord in this area. They would milk the building for all the money they could then let it go to foreclosure. As they come up on the second floor, Serena notices a man using some recreational drugs and walks over.

Serena asks in a strong voice if they often do this type of thing here while taking the badge off her belt and flashing it in the man's face. The man was a very old and looked like he was very sick because of his poor complexion and build. Malnourishment was the first thing that came to Serena mind. The man looked right at her with a serious look of concern. He then said in a loud, scared voice "No ma'am! I mean officer! I mean!" The man quickly runs down the stairs and Serena hears a door slam.

Andy smiles and proceeds up the stairs with Serena and when they get to the door, Andy knocks twice. The woman opens up the door as far as her door chain will allow her. Andy and Serena both show their badges. Andy explains they are detectives working on the case regarding her brother Zuriel. Lenore closes the door and Serena could hear her unlocking the door lock and chain. She opens the door and invites them into her apartment. As they walk in, Andy gives Lenore a big hug and offers his condolences on the loss of her brother. She explains she wants to make funeral arrangements but they won't tell her when the body will be let out of police custody. Andy explains that could take time depending on the length and case situation.

Lenore offers them a seat on her living room couch. Serena immediately jumps into the questions. "Do you know if your brother had any problems with anyone friends, co-workers, enemies or anything like that?" Lenore says "No, I don't think so. Zuriel was very quiet and to himself. He did not have many friends. I mean, we did not talk a whole lot about his friends or work. I know he started dating a new girl he met somewhere but she broke up with him shortly after a few dates."

Andy then asks with a sound of concern in his voice "Please is there anything else you can think of that would help us?" Lenore sits there pondering in thought then replies "No, not really but to tell you the truth this news was disturbing and has kind of thrown me off. If I remember anything I will call you. Andy puts his card down on the living room table and says "Well if you think of anything at all please don't hesitate to call me."

As Serena and Andy get in the car. Serena quickly comments on how they got no leads. Andy quickly replies and says "You get this sort of thing sometimes. Let's go back to the station and see what else we can turn up."

Once back at the station, Serena examines the body again. Jessica walks in the room and hands the blood work to Serena. Serena was very impressed at the speed of the results. She was guessing that part of the reason why the rush because of Andy's relationship with the victim. Serena looks down and examines the results.

Blood contains high levels of C14, H9 and Cl5 chemicals. Chemicals most commonly used in DDT and pesticides. High levels of insulin

Serena immediately looks at Jessica. She has a surprised look on her face as she explains that the victim was poisoned by pesticides. Jessica explains the tests normally take longer but this was an easy find. Serena then asks "What about high level of insulin?" Jessica replies back "I think he was a diabetic." Serena thinks to herself then announces out loud that explains all these little holes on his fingers testing his blood sugar.

Serena then proceeds up stairs to show this information to Andy. Andy is sitting at his desk. Serena explains to Andy that she received the test results and their victim was poisoned by pesticides. Andy gets up and puts his jacket on. He says tomorrow they can start checking out chemical manufacturing plants. He does not think there are many of them in the city. They might be able to get a lead off that.

Serena asks what Andy's plans are for the evening. He says he will be going to a parent teacher night at his son's school. She tells Andy to have fun and she will see him tomorrow.

Serena sits at her living room table of her small apartment. She unholsters her gun and unloads it, dropping the clip and clearing the chamber. Serena never had kids over her house but this was a habit she had picked up from her father watching him do this when she was a small girl.

She opens the fridge to find some leftover pizza to eat for dinner. Her dad had raised her the best he could. He was not a cook and took the liberty of passing that gene along to Serena. In her mind, when she saw a housewife cooking food she always thought in her head "Thanks dad." She had been raised on takeout and TV dinners. It was tough for her father. A single dad working a rotating shift was not easy. She never held it against him because he did his best as a father and he was great.

She looked to her left to the picture of her dad and her. He was holding her up on his shoulders. That was her favorite picture of the two of them. She had it blown up and placed in an 8 x 10 in frame she had made off an online craft store that said "Loved Father and Cop".

After eating, she sat on the couch to watch TV. The noise was mostly just to take her mind off the sound of emptiness. She lived alone and the TV helped drown out noise of neighbors, outside traffic and creaks from the apartment. As she looked at the TV, she felt her eyes get heavy as she dozed off to sleep.

CHAPTER 2

Serena wakes to the sound of a phone ringing. When she answers the phone, she immediately notices the voice on the other end is Andy's. She asks Andy what the emergency was that got her up an hour ahead of her alarm clock. He explains there was another murder last night and they believe the killer to be linked to the case they are already working on. Andy says he will pick Serena up right away. Serena says she will make haste and get ready.

Once they arrive on the scene, everything is already taped off with police tape. Serena had a quick flash back to when she was a beat cop. The yellow police tape that reads *Do Not Cross Crime Scene.* She often wondered how many miles of that tape she must have set up and unraveled while working as a "Baby in Blue" as the detectives had nicknamed her.

She was very much enjoying the role reversal of getting to walk under or around the tape rather than the actual setup and guard she was used to doing as part of her duties.

As she walks under the tape, she takes notice of the house. It was a beautiful home, very expensive. She was expecting that since this was a very high profile part of town. The only way anyone could afford a house in this neighborhood was to have a high level of income. The house was very modern, all glass and expensive furniture, with a gorgeous balcony that Serena admired.

As she starts to approach, a beat cop comes up on her and shakes her and Andy's hands. The officer's name was Simons. He was a tall African American man and very well built. Serena had seen him exercising at the gym at the precinct regularly. He explains that he was the first on the scene and had to break in the front door. The three officers begin to walk through the house. Andy asks who made the 911 call. Simons explains the neighbor saw the body this morning from her balcony. Andy asks where the body was found.

Just as he finishes his statement, they

arrive at the back door and notice a body floating in the pool of the house. Andy makes a comment telling Simons not to answer his previous question. They arrive just as the body is being taken out of the water. Serena walks over to examine the body. The first thing she notices is the bruises around his neck. The marks wrap completely around the neck. You could very easily tell the man had been strangled. As Serena walks around examining the pool, she can visibly see no murder weapon. She asks Simons to please have someone drain the pool so they can find the murder weapon. She tells them to keep their eyes open for wires, ropes or plastic bags. Anything that can be used as strangling device since that's how we know the victim was murdered.

Serena crouches down at the edge of the pool to looking for clues. She looks up to notice security cameras. She tells Simons to have someone find the camera server so Andy and she can review the tape. It would be a great to get a picture of the killer. Jessica continues to walk around the pool and examine things. She decides to sit down on a piece on lawn furniture that had a towel trapped over the top of the reclining chain. As she sits, she feels a book like object under her back. She also thought the object was a book due to the shuffling of pages she could hear. She immediately gets up and moves the towel to find a paperback book with a title *"Used To Be Me"*. She turns it over to see in red pen circled writing

"How Davis razorback jumping frogs can level six piqued gymnasts."

She immediately drops the book "Shit!" Andy and Serena come running over quickly "What's wrong?" "I touched evidence without gloves on!" Jessica immediately puts on her gloves and calls for an evidence bag. She places the book into the evidence bag. She hands the bag to Serena. Serena holds the bag up to the light and notices the sentence in red. She ponders for a minute about what it could mean. She looks over at Andy. "Any ideas on what it means?" Andy takes the bag into his own hand and looks at it and replies "No, Clue."

Andy handed the evidence back to Jessica. Serena and Andy make their way over to the body which is now fished out of the water and in a body bag. Andy unzips the body bag and immediately recognized the face. Andy takes a gasp and says "I know this guy!" Serena replies quickly and stunned hearing this news "Who is he?" Andy looks right at her "He is a lawyer. I knew him from a case we had worked a few months ago."

Serena sees the concern in Andy's face. Knowing one of the victims is a coincidence but not two in two days. That would be impossible. Andy walks away to look at pool. Serena knew this was just a distraction to buy himself time to compose himself and gather his thoughts on what he just saw in the body bag minutes ago.

Andy, after a few minutes, speaks to one of the other detectives. Apparently, there was evidence found in the house that is being sent to the lab. They would have to wait until results from the lab came in before they could chase any leads.

On the drive back to station, Andy was completely quiet. Serena knew Andy was concerned or going through the thoughts in his head about the case. She knew Andy was thinking of something. They had not knocked on any neighbors' doors or checked for any witnesses.

When they arrived, Serena went directly to her desk to investigate the lawyer they had just pulled out of the pool. Daren Davis was apparently a big shot defense attorney who had made his name by representing big time clients such as mob bosses and killers. He likes to live life to the fullest according to his most recent credit report.

He owned several high end sports cars, three half million dollar homes in United States and a single million dollar home on an island off of Italy. As Serena checked some of his recent credit card transactions, she knew he liked expensive clothing. His last purchase was at a Taylor's for over $2500 for a suit.

Andy had gone to talk to the District Attorney with his old partner about a case that had been in progress for well over 8 months. It was the last case worked with his old partner. Andy would be gone the rest of the day. It was about lunch time and Serena decided to take a trip to lunch. She figured she could stop by the attorney's office to see what files he had been working on, thinking it would lead to clues.

Serena grabbed her leather jacket and

headed out the door. She would have to take her own car since Andy and his old partner had taken the department issued Crown Vic they ride around in normally.

Serena drove a 4 year old Mustang. It was perfect for her as it was a two door and fast enough that she could get to crime scene in a rush. She stopped for a second cup of coffee and quick taco from a vender on the street.

When she arrived at law office, she noticed the office was on 15th floor of one of the most expensive spaces in Manhattan. When she walked in, the security for the building stopped her, she flashed her badge at them and they let her pass through with no issues.

She made her way into the law office and looked around. The place looked empty. The only person in this huge office space that could hold a dozen lawyers was one secretary. There was not a single lawyer in the entire place. She looked around and noticed how lavish the office looked. Expensive leather sofas in the waiting room, wall to ceiling glass doors engraved with the name of lawyers on them and what looked to be expensive conference rooms with expensive plasma TVs on the walls.

Serena looked at the secretary. She was a younger woman in her mid 30's with long curly red hair. It was obvious that she dyed it. She had long manicured nails and a nice blue blouse and short black skirt with thigh high heeled boots.

The women looked up as soon as Serena walks in the door and greets her in a welcoming voice. "Hello! Can I help you?" Serena showed her badge and said "I am one of the detectives handling the Darin Davis murder I need to see what cases Mr. Davis was working on." The secretary has a thoughtful look on her face. "I am not sure I can do that. Lawyer-client privilege protects Mr. Davis' files. I am going to have put you in touch with his paralegal." "Is there anyone else that works in this office?" Serena asked. "No just Mr. Davis, his paralegal and myself. We got this space after a tenant broke their lease. It's way more then we need but it's the Hilton compared to where we used to be." She says this while dialing the phone and then replies "Her phone went right to voicemail. I think she has it off. I know she had something in court today. Here is her card. Her name is Lesley."

Serena thanks the women and proceeds to leave the office. Heading back to her car, she pulls her phone out of her pocket. She had a department issued rugged flip phone. She never understood why the department issued her a "dumb phone" as she called it. Some of the detectives had iPhones but she had this. She carried her personal iPhone with her so she could check her email. She texted Andy *"Call me when you have a second."*

Every time she sent a text, she got annoyed having to tap the 1 multiple times for capital C then tap it again for an A. It always felt silly that she could not use her personal phone except to check emails but that was department rules. "Bureaucracy at its finest" she thought sarcastically.

As she got to the car, her phone vibrated. It was Andy. She flipped it open to answer "Hey partner. What's up?" Andy replied back with a laughing tone "I don't know. You wanted me to call you when I had second." "How's your old partner?" "He is well being him." Andy said very sarcastically "What's up?"

Serena replied, "I am trying to get a look at Davis case files. I got told we may not be able to as quickly as we like due to lawyer-client privilege. I have a number for his paralegal. She is my next call."

Andy sighs and says "If they don't play ball, we're going to need a warrant. If we need that, it will take time considering some of that information is sensitive and the court will want look over it. Let's hope it does not come to that or we could be working on this case a month from now." "That long Andy?!" "Yes, Serena. I have waited sometimes 2 months because what we're asking for requires someone having the free time to go through every file and case to make sure it's safe for us to look at. Our best bet is making nice with the paralegal." "I will talk to her see if I can get her to help us." Serena closed the phone ending the call.

She got in her Mustang, pulled the paralegal card out of her pocket and dialed the number. It went right to voicemail. She decided to leave a message. "This is Detective Serena Triton of NYPD. I am sorry about your boss but I am investigating his murder and need to talk to you about the cases he was working on. Please call me back at this number (Serena gives her cell phone number). Thank you." When leaving messages with witnesses or people she needed to speak to, she always used Detective Serena Triton rather than Detective Triton. She felt leaving a first name made her less intimidating to call back and people may return her calls quicker if they were not scared of her.

Serena looked at the screen of her phone. She still had quite a while left on her shift. She wanted to go interview the women that made the 911 call for the body in the park yesterday. When Serena called her yesterday, she told Serena to call back after noon as she would be off of work. Serena dialed the number she had in her notebook. The phone rang a few times and someone picked up. "Hello", a woman's voice responded. "Hi, this is Detective Serena Triton. Is this Gabriel?" "This is she." "I am calling you because you made the 911 call for the body in the park yesterday. Do you have few minutes just to answer a few questions?" Serena inquired. "Yes, sure. Not sure what I can tell you. I kind of just found the body there." "I just want to verify what time did you find the body?"

Serena could tell Gabriel was thinking "Around 7:30. Yes it had to be 'cause I walk through the park to get to work and I have to be at work at 8. I was running early so yes around 7:30." Serena asked, "Was there anyone else there around the body when you saw it" "No. No one but me. Am I a suspect?" Gabriel asked fearfully.

"No, you're not. I'm just asking some questions to gather information that's all. Nothing to worry about." Serena said soothingly. Is there anything else you could think of that might be useful to use?" Still with a nervous tone in her voice, Gabriel replied "No nothing I can think of. I am very sorry. I wish I could give you more." Serena replied, "Thank you very much Gabriel. You have my number if anything comes to mind. Please call me any time day or night."

Serena flipped the phone closed looking at her little notebook. She had roughly the time he was found but so far the case was pretty cold. She flipped the phone open again and called Jessica direct. She picked up "Forensics. This is Jessica." "Jess, it's Serena. Do you have anything back on that pool body yet?" Jessica replies "Nothing yet on blood work. I found another puncture wound on the neck. I am waiting for blood work to confirm anything." Serena fires back "Let me know."

Serena flips her phone closed and pulled out her iPhone sliding to unlock it, checking her email. She had her email setup to just show the headers. She would then click into an email to read the body if it was important. She had both her personal and work email accounts on her phone so she would see them all together. She saw that she had three new emails.

Your Time Warner Bill Has Been Paid
Your Carfax is ready - *spam*
Mandatory Health Care Get it Now - *spam*

Besides knowing her cable bill was paid nothing else was important. Serena decided it was time to head home for the day. The ride back to the station would take at least 40 minutes. It would be time to go home by then. She started her car and headed home.

CHAPTER 3

On the way home Serena decided she was not in the mood to cook or have leftovers. She decided to stop by the local cop bar. The bar was not just for cops but most cops hung out there. The food was good and a reasonable price for a cop's salary and had nice environment. The building had been condemned for years. It was one of the oldest buildings in this part of town but a young husband and wife took it over last year and made a go of it as successful entrepreneurs. "Good for them", she thought.

She parked around back and headed in the front door and as soon as she walked in she heard "Serena!" She looked around to see where the yelling was coming from. "Serena over here!" as young women waved.

Serena noticed right away it was her friend Hunter. Hunter was around the same age as Serena with bright blond hair and blue eyes. She and Serena had worked together when they were beat cops. Serena walked over and hugged Hunter. "How are you Hunter?" "I am fine. This is my boyfriend Todd and his friend Keith." Hunter said as she introduced the pair. "This is Detective Serena Triton of NYPD." Serena quickly comes back with "Serena is fine." as she giggles with Hunter "So Serena what you doing here?" says Hunter.

"I just got off. I am working a few cases today. Nothing too crazy. How are things at your new job?" Hunter was an FBI profiler. The two had met when Serena was taking her detective training and Hunter was finishing up her training for the FBI. They kept in touch regularly after they went their separate ways via Facebook posts and the occasional email.

"Great, I love it. So Keith here is single by the way and I know the last time we spoke you were in the market for a boyfriend." Serena gave a grin to Hunter and said "Way to be subtle." Keith chimes in "I had nothing to do with this I swear. Can I buy you a drink?" Serena replies back "No, but you can buy me something to eat. I am starving." Keith and Serena both made their way to their own table.

Serena ordered a cheese steak and cold soda. Keith ordered onion rings and a beer. Serena looks at Keith with a smile "You know I am a cop right. I don't want to arrest you for drunk driving." Keith smiles back "No, I walked here from my apartment. Drinking and walking is not a crime right?" Serena smiled at him "What do you do to pay the bills?" "I am a professor at a college. I teach English and writing courses. I am working on my master's as well."

Serena felt a little nervous. She was a detective and here she was sitting with a college professor. The only school after college she had attended after high school was the academy and her detective training.

As she looked at Keith, she found him very attractive. He had a well groomed beard, a short hair cut and was well built. Judging by his forearms, she could tell he worked out occasionally. He had brown hair and the most gorgeous eyes she had ever seen in her life. He was well spoken and seemed interested in her. He had not taken his eyes off her since they had sat down at the table.

As they sat there talking, Serena was doodling on her napkin. It was getting to her that two murders in two days had this mysterious code. Both codes had the victim's name in the writing. She wrote the first one on the napkin. *"Zuriel's Yelling Could Not Stop The Quick Brown Fox From Jumping Over The Dog"*

She continued to banter back and forth with Keith. She did not want to be rude and, well, it had been a while since she had any male companions besides Andy. When their food came, she stopped writing and ate, being very careful how she fed herself. She did not want look like a slob and turn off her new cute friend Keith.

Keith continued to talk to her about the subject of his master's degree and where he grew up along with the college he attended and other small talk. He had studied overseas and had traveled the country while in college. At times it made Serena wonder if she had missed out on the whole college experience and if it was something she should have pursued. But she was happy with her job and was enjoying Keith's stories and company. After they were done eating, the waiter took their empty plates away and Keith and Serena continued to talk.

Hunter came over after quite a while. "I am leaving you two love birds. I have early day tomorrow." Serena hugged Hunter goodbye as she and her boyfriend left to head home. The two had lived together for years Serena wondered if Hunter's boyfriend would ever pop the question. Serena turned her attention back to Keith. "So Keith, why no girlfriend? A young, smart, successful guy like you could have tons of girls." Keith just smiled back. "I am only in hopes to find the one. She just has not come along yet. You?"

Serena looked back at him with a smirk, liking his answer "It's tough. This job is not a 9-5 and being a woman on top of it? How do you raise kids and all when you never know when you could be called out or heaven forbid killed in the line of duty?" "I understand that Serena but whoever you get with should understand that." Serena just shrugged "I know but in my head I feel bad for the other person and don't want to put them through that. Hey, it's getting late. I better get going Keith." Keith replied "Of course. Let me just pay the bill and then I will walk you to your car."

Serena was taken with him. He was so

sweet. How he wanted to be a gentleman and walk her to the car. It was romantic. He wanted her to feel safe walking to her car. She really did not need him to as she had a gun and police training. She was in the mood to feel a little girly and having a big, strong, handsome man walk her to her car was a nice feeling for a change.

Keith paid the bill then dropped a cash tip on the table. He grabbed his coat and followed her as they walked towards the door. Keith quickly said with some wit "I usually would offer to help you with your coat but you never took it off." Serena was still trying to savor the moment of him walking her to the car just said "It's a bit chilly in here." She did not want to point out the fact she left her leather coat on because she was a cop and was trying to hide her gun and badge.

As they got to her car, Keith became a bit of a typical man's man and got a bit excited "Wow! You drive a Mustang? This is a fast car for a....." He paused. Serena finished his sentence "For a girl." Keith stuttered "No! I mean... I didn't..." Serena quickly replied "It's fine." She actually found it cute to a certain degree. She then said with a little nervous tremble in her voice, "Do you want my number?" Keith replies "Yes, please!"

Serena opens her can and grabs one of her cards out of glove box. Here is my number and that's my cell phone for work. I always have it on so text or call me." Just as she reaches in her pocket for her phone, she pulls out the napkin she was writing on. She opens it up to see what it was and before she has a chance to put it away, Keith chimes in, "That's cool a pangram." Serena quickly replies back in shock "Wait! What's that? Explain it please."

Keith goes into an explanation about what a pangram is and how it works. 'A pangram is a Greek word for every letter or holoalphabetic sentence for a given alphabet. It pretty much is a sentence using every letter of the alphabet at least once. Pangrams have been used to display typefaces, test equipment and develop skills in handwriting, calligraphy and keyboarding. I teach a chapter of it in my class. Serena was floored. This was no coincidence. The killer was leaving a calling card. He or she was the pangram killer.

Serena kissed Keith good bye on the cheek and said she would see him again. She wanted to get home and get a good night's rest because tomorrow she wanted to get to office early to tell everyone what she had found out. They were looking for a serial killer.

CHAPTER 4

When Serena's alarm went off, she jumped out of bed. She wanted to get down to the station as soon as possible. She wanted to talk to Andy and check the toxicology reports which should have been in by now. She jumped in shower real quick; blow dried her hair and was out the door with a few minutes to spare to grab a coffee at local vender.

She got into the office before Andy. This was unusual as he was an early riser with 2 small children at home. She wanted to check on toxicology reports. She walked over to where the reports usually are but nothing was in yet. Serena asked one of her fellow detectives who was sitting at his desk in his cubicle. "Excuse me where's the toxicology reports? They should be in by now" He replied back "They're going to be a little late today. Jess had a sonogram this morning for her baby. Once she gets in, she will get them to us."

Just as Serena sat back at her desk to check on the overnight reports, her cell phone vibrated. It was Lesley from the attorney's office. "This is Serena" "Is this Detective Serena Triton of NYPD?" Serena could tell by the voice that this was a young woman about her age. "This is she. How can I help you?" "This is Lesley from the law offices of Davis. I got your message and I want you to know I think we can help you out with those case files you requested." Serena was happy. "That's great! When can I pick them up?" Lesley replied back in a soft tone "Here is the thing, some of those files are protected by lawyer-client privilege but this is what I can do for you detective. I will go through the files and write down the names of the clients we were representing and the charges they are facing. That's public knowledge. If one interests you, let me know and I will bring the file down to you and we can go over it together." Serena replied back "That will work for me. When can I get this information?" Lesley replies "Later today if you want pick them up." Serena replies back "That's fine. This is my cell. Let me know."

As she was talking, Andy walked in the door and sat down at his deck with a cup of coffee that he had just gotten from squad room coffee pot. "That sounds promising." He said when she hung up. Serena nodded and said "They're going to give us a list of filenames and charges we can look at that and go from there." "That sounds good to me Serena. How about we go back by Davis's neighborhood and knock on some doors?" "I am up for that. Let's go." Serena quickly logged in to her computer and pulled up pictures of Zuriel and Davis and printed them on her color printer. She grabbed the pictures off the printer and headed to the crown Vic.

They arrived at the neighborhood and cruised around the block a few times to see what were the best neighbors to ask in hopes of getting a good lead. The first thing Serena noticed when they were cruising around the block is how expensive and lavish all the houses in the area were. She could tell none of these people were cops.

They parked the car and headed to the

first house they chose. Serena knocked on the door and a man answered. He was middle-aged with grey hair and was well groomed. She could tell his polo shirt was not something you get at the local Wal-Mart. Andy lifted his badge and introduced himself and his partner. Serena then showed the pictures and asks if he recognizes the victims and does he know if they had any strange activity or people in the area in the last few days. He says no to all their questions. It's obvious he did not know the victims or hardly anyone in neighborhood.

They knock on the next house and the same process leads to no results. They knock on a few more doors with the same results happening. After almost two hours, Andy and Serena knew this was going nowhere fast. While they were walking to the car, Serena's phone buzzes. It was Lesley. Serena picks it up. "Hello this is Serena." "Hi Serena, this is Lesley. I have your information. I can send it by courier or can you can come pick it up?" "My partner and I will pick it up shortly." Serena flips the phone closed.

It was a short drive to the lawyer's office. Serena wondered how many times Davis had made the trip from his home to the office. When Serena went upstairs to the office, the secretary handed her a large envelope. As they drive to the station, Serena opens the envelope and sees a list of names and charges.

James Edwards - Drunk and disorderly
Steven Clark - Child support pass due
David Markis - Domestic dispute
Laura Lenzo - Domestic dispute
Rita Clark - Prostitution
Michael Rice – Murder (Prosecutor)

As Serena read last line, Michael Rice jumped out at her. She looked at Andy and asked "When were you going to tell me that Davis was the defense attorney working your old case with your partner?" Andy looks right at her. "It's not relevant and he was not the defense attorney. He was the prosecutor." Serena looked back at Andy. "That does not make sense. Why the hell would a known defense attorney be working for the district attorney office?" Andy replies back, still keeping his eyes on the road to avoid an accident, "Because he was hired by the district attorney to work the case in place of the DA." Serena at this point has a look of confusion on her face "Why? That still does not make any sense at all."

Andy jumps in, "Yes it does Serena. The DA is up for reelection this year and why would he risk his reputation and good conviction rate on a high profile case like the Rice case? Hire an outsider; let him work the case. If he fumbles it, you declare mistrial and then he handles it after his election is over. It's politics." Serena had a very disgusted look on her face as they pull into the station parking lot. She holds up the file and asks "Why have me get this information when you have a copy of the file we need?"

Andy looks back at her as he throws car into park. "I am sorry I did not tell you but I know you would figure out the connection sooner or later especially when you called from the law office. I have something else to tell you. Come inside with me and we will open the file."

As Serena walks through the parking lot, she pulls out her iPhone to check her email. The first email catches her attention.

Blood Work Report on Your Desk Jessica :)
Win A Free Trip - *spam*
Concert in Town

As she read her three emails, she was happy the blood work was in and excited to see one of her favorite bands was in town. Maybe she would ask Keith to go with her if he liked rock music.

As they get to Andy's desk, he pulls out the Rice file. "So here is the deal with Rice." Andy has almost a narrator tone. "Him and a few of his buddies decided to knock off a police warehouse that had something in the realm of 3 million in cash in it from a heroin bust several months prior." Serena quickly jumps in, "How did homicide get involved?"

Andy says with a little bit of friendly sarcasm in his voice, "Let me finish. During the break in, one cop who was on watch that night got killed and another wounded. We got Rice because he took a bullet in the leg and one in the shoulder and was down for the count. The other two suspects got away and we could never find them. Rice is going down for the murder of a cop but has agreed to give the state evidence along with the names of the other two involved in exchange for no death penalty. With Davis dead, there will be a new lawyer put on the case but I can imagine the same terms will apply."

Serena was curious now "How the heck did they break into a police warehouse?" Andy answers, "These guys had full on tactical gear and automatic weapons. Rice has some military experience. Perhaps the other people did as well or he trained them. I don't know. We never had luck hunting down the other two suspects." Serena then puts her hand to her chin in thought. "How would they know about the drug money? We don't disclose in the media where we store that stuff."

Andy replies, "You're right, we don't. So it could have been an inside job. But there are other people that have access to that warehouse on the civilian side. The warehouse manager, a few of the workers, the cleaning crew and maintenance crew, just to name a few. It could have been any one of them that mentioned to friend over a beer or football game that we had 3 million in cash there waiting to be taken."

Serena sits on Andy desk "I have not been totally honest with you. I had a suspicion that the cases were connected. Those notes we've been finding with the body? They're pangrams. The killer is marking his or her territory." Andy looks at her. "How did you figure out it was a pangram?"

Serena reaches for the toxicology report she sees on her desk. "My new boyfriend is a teacher. He noticed it on napkin I wrote it on." Just as she said that, she was taken aback. She had addressed the guy she had just met last night as her boyfriend. She kind of liked the way it sounded.

Andy leans back in his chair. "Really, so who is the future Mr. Triton?" Serena looks up from her files with serious sort of joking look "You don't know him." Serena followed that up with "We definitely know the murders are linked. Same pesticides in the blood as before." She hands the file to Andy and he reads the report. Serena replies "I will setup the murder book."

Serena sat at her desk most the rest of the day working on the murder book. In law enforcement, the term murder book refers to the case file of a murder investigation. Typically, murder books include crime scene photographs and sketches, autopsy and forensic reports, transcripts of investigators' notes and witness interviews. The murder book encapsulates the complete paper trail of a murder investigation, from the time the murder is first reported through the arrest of a suspect.

Serena was thinking about how recently one homicide detective left a murder book at local cafe in New York. Law enforcement agencies typically guard murder books carefully, and it is unusual for civilians to be given unfettered access to these kinds of records, especially for unsolved cases. This particular book was picked up by, of all people, a New York Times reporter trying to make a name for herself. After a four page article in the paper, she was promoted to editor and the detective linked to the mistake was demoted to the archive room. Serena often wondered how bad you would need to mess up to be fired. Most times when cops did something really bad, rather than fire them, they get a job in the cage or typing reports.

Serena was pulled out of her daydream by her phone vibrating. She picked it up, looked at the number and saw it was Keith. She wanted to impress him. She flipped the phone open and answered "Detective Serena Triton NYPD." "Hi, it's Keith. Did I catch you at bad time?" Serena smiled. "No, I am free for a few minutes." Keith replied, "Would you like to grab dinner tonight?" Serena was not feeling in the mood to go out. She had always felt honesty was best thing in any relationship especially one starting out in the early phases. "I am not really in mood to go anywhere tonight." Keith, a little surprised, made a counter offer. "How about if I come over to your place and cook?" Serena was a bit taken by his offer. She happily agreed and gave him her address and a time to come over for dinner. She looked at the time. It was about the end of her shift. If she rushed home now, she would have time to clean the place up before Keith came over.

CHAPTER 5

As Serena came home, she put her keys down took, her jacket off and unloaded her gun and put it in her hiding spot in the dresser for safe keeping. She then put the loaded magazine on top of bookshelf in her living room in a music box her dad had gotten for her as a little girl. She turned the dial on the music box a few times to hear the sound. It took her back to her childhood and made her think about her dad.

She picked up his picture and looked at in her special frame. Her dad had died over a year ago from hardening arteries. Over time, this complication can block the arteries and cause fatal issues throughout the body. In her father's case, when arteries are narrowed by fatty deposits, you have a greater risk for developing blood clots. Your blood can carry these clots until they become lodged in narrow spaces. When this happens, the clot can significantly or completely block the blood supply to parts of the body. Her father suffered a heart attack and died in his sleep. She was devastated. He was the only family she had and she missed him greatly. She knew in her heart her dad would approve of Keith.

With the remaining time before Keith arrived, she got changed out her work clothing and put on something sexier. A V neck blouse and jean skirt with high heel boots. She looked at herself in mirror. She thought to herself, "Sexy and not too dressy... Perfect." She went in the bathroom quick to check and fix her makeup, brush her hair and teeth.

She was walking out of bathroom when her doorbell rang. "Perfect timing", she thought. She walked over and looked through the peephole. "Cop instinct always has you wanting to know who was on the other end of a door before opening it", she thought. It was Keith as expected. He had a paper bag in his arms with groceries in it. She checked herself one more time in the mirror by the door quickly then welcomed Keith into her home.

Keith comes in the door hugs Serena hello and walks over to the table and puts down the bag of groceries. He quickly goes into his meal plans. "I make a fabulous chicken cordon bleu. I hope you like chicken. I should have asked." Serena has her hands folded down by her waist with a big smile and slowly walked towards the kitchen. She says "Chicken is fine."

Serena pulls the pans out for him that he requests and Keith goes to town cooking away. The paper bag he brought was like a magic trick. Everything he needed came out of there; the oil for the pan, seasoning, chicken, ham, cheese. At the bottom were a dozen beautiful roses and he handed them to Serena after he set up dinner and was waiting for it to cook.

She smiled and kissed him on the cheek and thanked him for being so sweet. She put her nose close to the roses and smelled them. They smelled great like he did. She was not sure what it was but it was very nice smelling cologne. She reached in one of the cabinets by her sink to find a vase. She cut the bottom of the flowers and put them in water. She placed them on the living room table where they would be eating.

She decides to take it a step further. She went into the living room and opened a door under a hutch and pulls out two candle sticks with long white candles in them. She sets them down on the table, one on each side of the flowers. She goes into the top silverware drawer of the kitchen and grabbed a pack of matches. She opens the pack strikes a match and lights both candles. She waves the match out and puts the pack back into the drawer.

She leans on the table in a somewhat of a sexy pose and holds her hand up in a gesturing manner "Candle light dinner and flowers. Now it's a date." Keith smiles as he finishes up dinner and portions it into the plates for the two of them. Serena sits down at the table while Keith brings over both plates and places hers in front of her and places his own on his place setting. Serena goes to get up. "Let me get us some drinks."

Keith stops her. "Sit down. I have it." He walks over to the kitchen and takes two wine glasses off the shelf and puts them on the table. He reaches deep into his paper bag and brings out a bottle of white wine. He even has his own corkscrew. He opens the bottle and pours them both a glass of wine.

While they're eating, Serena fires off some small talk questions that she was curious about. Questions along the lines of "What sports do you like?" "What car do you drive?" and "Where did you learn to cook with this?"

These were her top three piquing her curiosity. Finding out Keith liked baseball was a plus. She enjoyed the sport and the Yankees were easy enough to get to in a short ride from her apartment. Keith liked the Yankees so Serena hoped the two of them could catch a game sometime.

Keith was apparently not a car guy as he drove a two year old Chevy Malibu and from their conversation, had never even changed a tire until recently. Serena was ok with that. His intellect and good looks made up for his lack of mechanical skills. She knew one thing; he would not be fixing his car anytime soon.

The cooking question was interesting to Serena. Keith had taken a few cooking lessons at the college where he taught. Keith said it gave him something to do at nights and he thought it would be a good place to meet girls. He just did not expect them all to be two or three times his age. The story made Serena laugh thinking about walking into a class on the first day thinking to see drop dead gorgeous women and you get women old enough to be your mom.

As they chatted, they finished up their meal and cleared the table. Keith offered to do the dishes while Serena dried them all and put them away in the kitchen. After Serena was done drying the dishes, she filled both their wines glasses and invited Keith to sit on the couch.

Keith took a look around her living room, noticing the bookshelves that were only a few feet away. He started to read the titles of the books off to her. She laughed and asked him to stop. Keith smiled "Are you looking for romance in your life?" "I am single woman, living alone. I am entitled to some sleazy romance novels once in a while, plus when I am on a long stake out, they help the time go by." Keith reads some more titles. "Are you into vampires?" "It depends on the book and author. Most of those I got from a neighbor down the hall when she was moving out. Again, I have long stakeouts sometimes and it makes time go by. Some of them are kind of raunchy but most are pretty action packed. One is about a detective who is a woman and vampire. There is a whole series of those. They're fun to read."

Keith stands up and pulls one book off the shelf "What's this?" He flips it over and reads the title out loud. "Understanding And Reading The Crime Scene". He holds the book up to show her while taking a sip of his wine. "I had to read that when I went to the academy for my detective training. It's a textbook of sorts." Keith goes book by book, checking title names and keeping track with his finger. "They say you can tell a lot about a woman by what she reads. This is quite a collection. Ever think of going to a book club?" "I would if I had the time but I don't. My work schedule is pretty nuts." Keith looks at Serena with sarcastic grin. "Yet you made time for me." Serena gives it right back. "Was a slow day. What can I say?"

They both laugh. Keith sits down next to Serena. She puts her head on his shoulder and places her hand on his chest. Keith looks at his watch. "I am sorry. I have to go. I have an early class and I am filling in for someone who says she has a doctor's appointment but probably just wants to sleep. You can never trust that people are who they say they are." He laughs "That's proper English from a teacher. I think the wine is hitting me." Serena asks "Are you ok to drive home?" Keith fires back "Yes, I am fine, really. I was just kidding. I guess I should know better than to kid around about that."

Keith gets his jacket on and opens the door, kisses Serena on the cheek and thanks her for her company. As Serena closes the door, she hears him walking down the hall. She locks it and turns around to lean against it pushing her head back all the way until it hits the door. She stands there for a minute and just ponders about her future with him. She was in love. She knew it and liked it.

CHAPTER 6

Serena got into the office early. She was going through the murder book, making sure everything was there and nothing was left out. She made copies of toxicology reports, pictures and typed all her notes on the case. She liked to make these books look as professional as possible considering her boss and other detectives were going to read it at some point.

Just as she took her notes off the printer on her desk, she saw Jessica walking over to the coffee pot for a cup of decaf coffee. Serena, feeling a bit chatty, asked "How's that decaf?" Jessica just smiled. "I can't wait till this kid comes out. He kept me up all night kicking. Then, to top it off, I get no caffeine. I love when people say being pregnant does not change their life. That's BS." They laughed and Jessica continued, "I am also wearing heels today. I should have my head examined wearing heels at 8 months pregnant." Again, both girls laughed.

Serena then asked "Jess, I got question for you about the toxicology report. It shows pesticides. Are these off the shelf?" Jessica replies "Usually the exterminators mix the recipe themselves. I don't know if there's a way to get them together. You can buy the stuff online." Serena replies, "That stinks. I was hoping to call around today and get a hit but it's going to be impossible especially if you can buy the stuff online." Jessica gave a look of disappointment then headed down the stairs to her lab to work.

Serena went back to work on the murder book. The one thing she was going to need to do was to get inventory of Zuriel's crime scene. She went down to archives and asked for evidence for her case. She signed the log book and brought the box back to her desk. She put on gloves and started going through the box item by item. She pulled out his iPhone which had a dead battery. She was going to have the technology forensics team look at this to see what data they could get off it and if it might be useful. She reached down into her purse and took out a charging cable. She plugged it into an outlet and let it charge. She just wanted to take a quick peek before she handed the phone over. It would be a while before she got it back.

The next items were his watch and a ring. Both looked normal enough and were insignificant. She logged them into the inventory sheet in the book. What she thought was kind of sad was most places had forensics teams that logged evidence in the murder book but not her precinct. With all the cutbacks in 2008, it forced the detectives to do these kinds of things.

The next item she pulled out was his wallet. She opened it and went through it. Nothing important grabbed her attention at first. A glance showed seventy two dollars in cash. Apparently the killer was not concerned about money. Next were his driver's license, debit card, health insurance card, and a few credit cards. A business card for Manhattan Porsche, however, snagged her attention. It stood out as Zuriel was a level two detective, just like Andy.

Andy was making around 75,000 a year. This was a modest salary for a cop but the benefits outweighed the salary.

Serena picked up her phone to text Andy. *"Call me."* Andy was meeting the new prosecutor assigned to the case. Apparently the DA's office wanted to get Rice this deal before he changed his mind. Her phone rang a few seconds after she sent the text. She answered the phone. "That was fast", she said kind of shocked. He returned the call so quick. "I am waiting for the DA's office to decide who is going to handle the case. I am going to be a while today."

"No big deal Andy. Just a couple questions. You knew Zuriel. Was his family wealthy at all? Did he get some inheritance? Ever hit it big on the lottery or anything like that?" Andy with a certain tone says "Zuriel! God no. He spent his life in foster care with no family, no nothing. Why? " Serena replied back, trying not to give everything away. "Nothing, just following a lead. I will explain later." "Serena, I feel bad you are doing all the work on this case. I will make it up to you sometime." Serena replies back with the comment of "Like that's going to happen anytime soon."

Serena flipped the phone closed. She
decided to call the salesman on the card to ask
a few question. She dialed the number on her
cell. A woman answered the phone.
"Manhattan Porsche. How can I help you?"
Serena replied "Yes, Hi. Is Brian in please?"
The woman replied "No, he on a test drive. Can
I take message?" Serena told the woman who
she was and asked to have Brian call her back
as soon as possible.

Serena noticed the iPhone was now
charged and operational. She was hoping the
phone did not have a password. She lifted it up
and it said **"Hello."** "Hmmm…" Serena thought
to herself. "That's interesting. Why would the
phone say that?" She went to the next screen.
"Select your language and country." She hit
next again. **"Get online and choose Location
Services."** She hit next again. **"Set up Touch
ID and create a passcode."** She hit skip.
**"Sign in with your Apple ID and set up
iCloud Drive."** She hit skip again. **"Choose
settings for app analytics and display
resolution."** She selected Finish and realized
the phone was acting like it was like brand new
out of the box. She checked the contacts,
recent messages and photos. There was

nothing even resembling usage. Even if Zuriel had gotten a new phone, he would have restored his phone from his iCloud backup. Whoever killed Zuriel must have wiped his phone.

Serena knew the data was not gone forever. Forensics could work with Apple to get the data but that would take time and a subpoena. Serena went to Apple's website and looked up their procedures for law enforcement. She found this on the site.

"We believe security shouldn't come at the expense of individual privacy. We regularly receive requests for information about our customers and their Apple devices from law enforcement. We want to explain how we handle these requests. When we receive information requests, we require that it be accompanied by the appropriate legal documents such as a subpoena or search warrant. We believe in being as transparent as the law allows about what information is requested from us. We carefully review any request to ensure that there's a valid legal basis for it. And we limit our response to only the data law enforcement is legally entitled to for the specific investigation."

What that meant to her was she was not going to get the data today or tomorrow to follow this lead. She got up to fill her coffee cup. She needed a little pick me up with everything going on. A little caffeine with cream and sugar always did the trick.

Her phone buzzed. It was Keith. The timing of text was perfect. *"Do you want have dinner tonight? :)"* The smiley face at the end was a nice touch but she was not sure she could make dinner. The morning was pretty spent and she had a lot paperwork to do on old cases. Dinner was out tonight. Her phone buzzed again and she recognized the number. It was the car dealership calling back. She answered "Detective Serena Triton." "Hi, Detective Triton. This is Brian from Manhattan Porsche. What can I do for you?" "Hi Brian. Thank you for calling me back. I have a few questions about a person who was looking to buy a car and was hoping you could answer them for me." "Of course Detective but I have to tell you, I am uncomfortable doing this over the phone. I would much rather meet in person." Serena replied "I can come down if you would like?" Brian replied "Please do. I will be here all day then I am off tomorrow." Serena came back with an assuring tone in her voice "I will be down to see you today."

Serena looked at the clock. She was going to have drive to Manhattan from where she was. It was not a long drive but she could swing by Keith for a quick lunch or coffee on the way back. She texted Keith "*Sorry no dinner. Want to grab a quick coffee after class?*" She debated about putting xoxox after her message but thought it might have been too soon for that in their relationship. She packed up the rest of the evidence into the box. She would finish the inventory for the murder book later. Right now she had to chase a lead.

She checked the box back into inventory and headed out to the parking lot of the station to get her car. Andy had the crown Vic so she was driving her Mustang. It was no big deal for her. She liked her car and did not mind driving it around on a nice day.

CHAPTER 7

As Serena pulls into the car dealership, she remembers all the fun she had when she bought her Mustang six months ago when she got her promotion. The car was not new but it was something she always wanted and she could afford it with the new raise.

She pulled into a parking space in front of the door and got out of her car. Not even a minute after getting out, a few salesmen on the lot were walking towards her and right then she knew the stereotype about women entering a car dealership were true.

She was a young healthy, good looking woman in her late 20's and driving a sports car. Salesmen saw dollar signs when they spotted her getting out of her Mustang. She figured she would have a little fun and show them her badge. They all immediately stopped working towards her and just waved. Serena got a bit of a laugh out of picking on the salesmen.

She walked inside again and showed her badge to the secretary and explained she was here to see Brian. The secretary walked into one of the glass offices, said something Serena could not hear and out came the person she assumed was Brian.

He was a short guy, only about 5 feet 8 inches tall and in a suit and tie. He had spiky, well-groomed hair and a goatee. He came over, introduced himself, shook Serena's hand and invited her into his office. As they walk to his office, Serena looked around. This car dealership had amazing, lavish glass offices, marble floors in every room and, from what she could tell, a bidet in bathroom. She was thinking to herself, "I guess when you sell cars that are more than what a cop makes in a year, you can afford this kind of operation."

Brian sat down behind his desk and Serena sat across in the chair. She made sure to show her badge and credentials to him. She started talking. "I found a business card from your company in wallet of a murder victim." She takes the card out that is now in an evidence bag and shows him. She then pulls out a photo of Zuriel. "Do you recognize this man?" Brian asks if he can see the picture more closely. She hands him the picture. "Oh, yeah! I remember this guy. He looked at a 911 Turbo; even test drove it as well." Serena response interested now. "So you remember the encounter?" Brian starts taking on a salesman voice. "Of course I remember. He was looking at the 911 Turbo with 520 horsepower, 6000 - 6500 rpm, 195 mph top speed… Yes I remember." Serena cuts him off. "Is there any reason why you remember this so clearly? You must deal with lots of customers a day. Why does this one stick out to you?" Brian leans back in his chair. "Detective he looked at an almost $210,000 car. It's one of the most expensive cars on the lot. My commission would have been 25% of that. Trust me, you don't forget a big number like that."

Serena knew that everyone is generally raised to not trust salesman, especially car salesman, but he seemed to be telling the truth from what she could tell. "Do you know how he was paying for this?" Brian opens a file on his desk and pulls out a paper and reads it. "According to this, he was going to pay cash. He said he had fallen into a little money recently. I did not question it. We generally don't on a cash deal." Serena then stood up "Well, thank you for your time." Brian quickly stands up in a sign of chivalry. "I wish I could have been more of help. That's really all I know. By the way, I saw you pull up in Mustang. Can I interest you in a free test drive of an on sale model?"

Serena just put her hand up in a gesture to say stop, put her card down on his desk and walked out the door to her Mustang. As she got in her phone, buzzed it was a text from Keith. "*Sure, I am done for day. I am at the coffee shop grading papers. When are you coming?*" She texted back, "*On my way.*"

As she got in the car and pulled out of the dealership, she called her partner and he picked up on the first ring. "Hey Serena. What's going on?" "I followed up a lead today. Our victim Zuriel apparently went to buy a six figure sports car not too long before his death. He told the dealer he fell into a little money." Andy exclaimed, "Wow! None of us make that kind of money." Serena cuts him off. "Another thing.

His phone was wiped clean." She could hear shock in Andy's voice. "But wait, why would someone wipe the phone? That does not make sense unless they did not want us to find something. Did you give the phone to digital forensics?" Serena replies "No, I was too busy. Could you do it? Are you at the office?" Andy replied, "Yes, I am going through the evidence now for the murder book. I will bring this down to them before I leave. Also, they completed the search of Davis's house and besides finding some weird sex toys and marijuana under the bed, the place turned up clean."

Serena was hoping for more than that. While she did get lucky today, she hoped tomorrow would be better. "How did you make out on the Rice case?" she asked? "They sent the Assistant District Attorney there today. No more outside contractors for this case. They want put this to bed. Apparently, Rice gave up some information and it looks like he is going to get a better deal than he was originally going to get." "Figures." Serena said sarcastically. "Well, he is still going to spend the rest of his life in prison. But, if he cuts a deal, he gets to do his first year in state then they're going to send him to federal. They're supposed to transfer him tomorrow if not day after." "Of course. It's easier doing time in state than federal." Serena says. "Exactly." Andy says. Serena, at this point, had moved through traffic quick. She was at the coffee shop now. "Listen Andy, I am going to jet. I am meeting someone. Please don't forget that phone." Andy replies, "I got it."

Serena flips the phone closed. She can see Keith sitting at one of the tables drinking what looked like a medium coffee and was grading papers. She thought that's what he was doing anyway judging by the red pen in his hand.

She got out of the car and walked into the coffee shop. She walked to the table and sat down across from Keith. He looked up and said "I am sorry. I did not hear you come in. Can I get you a coffee?" She smiled and replied, "Yes please, light and sweet like my men." Keith started to walk away then it hit him. He turned around and smiled.

While Keith was at the counter ordering her coffee, she looked over what he was grading. Most of these papers were on symbols and mythology. It was something she was interested in but knew very little about.

Keith came back over and put the coffee down in front of her. "Thank you Keith." "No problem, my pleasure. Glad you could make it on short notice." Keith says as he pulls his chair out and sits back down. "What you grading?" Serena asks with a curious tone. Keith closes the binder. "Nothing really just some stuff I have to grade for my classes. While I was waiting for you, I figured I would get some work done. How was your day?" Serena leads with "Someone tried to sell me a Porsche?" Keith looked shocked and said "Um… wow!" "I was chasing a lead today that brought me to a car dealership. It was all nothing to shake a stick at, just cop stuff." Keith smiled and said "I find your job interesting and exciting." Serena looks back at Keith. With those eyes, she felt like he was looking into her soul. "It's different everyday but you are the one educating the youth of America." Keith fires back "The ones that fail are the ones you end up chasing."

They both laughed. Serena really enjoyed his company. Even though they did not know each other too well, it was obvious they had something. "I almost did not come see you tonight." Serena says this while moving her long hair out of her face to see Keith better and for him to get a better look at her. Keith eyes open wide and he smiled. "Why? Did I do something?" Using a hair tie, Serena smiled, and pulled her hair back into a ponytail. "I just got off work. Look at me, I am a mess." Keith shrugged and said "Well, if you think this is a mess, I am afraid to see what a wreck looks like." "You know I can arrest you right?" Keith smirked and asked "Will there be handcuffs involved?" Serena rolls her eyes. "What is it with you men and wanting us female cops to handcuff you?"

They both laugh again and smile. It was obvious they were both feeling more comfortable around each other. She felt could be herself around him. She did not have to be fake and neither did he. They both, for the moment, were the right fit.

Just as she started to settle in, her phone vibrated. She pulled it out and saw it was Andy. "Andy, what's up?" "Serena, I just got a call from dispatch. We got another murder. This time it's the Assistant DA."

CHAPTER 8

Serena felt bad leaving Keith. He understood it was her job and he had his hands full grading papers anyway. This time, the murder was different. From what she got over the phone, the murder took place in a parking garage and from the chatter she heard over the police scanner she had in her car, it was messier than all the others.

Serena pulled into the parking garage. The cop holding the scene needed to see her badge and ID since she was not in a department issued car. She held up the information the office read it and waved her through.

The parking garage was a private

garage that was rented by the courthouse and DA's office for off street parking. As she pulled up the crime scene, she put the car in park and got out. Her first instinct was to check out the corners of the garage to see if there were any cameras. She quickly swept her gaze over the area and found none. She saw where Andy was standing and headed towards the crime scene. From what she could tell, the Assistant DA was laying face down. His blood was all over the floor and splattered all over his car and the surrounding walls. The car was a fairly new, black Lexus. On the front windows, written in white marker, was

"Pack my box with five dozen liquor jugs ADA."

Serena put on her rubber gloves and squatted down to examine the body. She could tell from the head trauma that the cause of death was blunt force trauma with some kind of heavy object. Serena notices all the blood splatter again and it convinced her that this was an extremely hard hit to the head.

Serena stands up and looks at the driver side car window. It was broken and she assumed with the same tool used in the murder. Serena walks over the car to see there is no blood or brain matter in the car. That must mean who ever kill the ADA must have made him get out of the car first.

Serena makes eye contact with Andy "No security cameras, how convenient." Andy replies while shaking his head, "I noticed that also when I arrived." Serena walks over to Andy so they don't have to yell. "Who found the body?" "Another attorney on his way out for the day." "Can we speak with him?" Serena asked. "Not now we can't. Paramedics had to give him a sedative. I guess this shook him up a bit." Serena starts looking around the crime scene. "Where is forensics?" Andy replies, "From what I got, Jessica overdid it at the gym in the station and started cramping up. She is in hospital. They're sending someone else from a different homicide team. They should be here soon."

Serena walks over to the body and squats down to take a closer look. "Andy, there is not puncture wound anywhere on the neck. This does not fit the killer's normal pattern. Someone must have gone wrong on this one." Andy looks and nods. "I was thinking same thing. Why blunt force trauma to the head?

Definitely not the pattern we have seen. The last two murders were clean and planned. This one is messy." Serena continues to look. "No one has come forward to say they saw anything as far as we know?" Andy replies "No, but I already called the local media for them to run the homicide tip number. We may get lucky." Serena, examining the wound on the head, turns to Andy and says "He or she hit him from behind. Look at the point of impact." She pointed but made sure not to touch the body until it was processed.

Andy again nods, crossing his arms. "All the victims have been men and all tied to the Rice case except for the first murder." Serena was standing up again. "Yeah, I know. That's the only one that out place. I bet if we look deep enough we will find him connected somehow." Andy looks at Serena. "Maybe we should call Rice's attorney and see if we can question him. Rice can probably shed some light on things."

Just then it hits Serena "Zuriel was one of the guys involved in the robbery. They made off with the cash right?" Andy says "Yes all of it." Serena then says, "He got killed for trying to buy that sports car and sending up a red flag.

The two attorneys got killed because Rice told them who the third person in robbery was for the plea agreement. This has got to be the third man covering his tracks." Andy looked at her with shock in his face "Your idea makes sense. In the morning we have to go see Rice. If your theory is correct we could finally end this murder spree."

By the time the forensic team got there and processed the scene, it was almost 5 am. Serena knew that Andy was coming in early to call Rice's defense attorney and get him in loop of how they wanted to question Rice.

Instead of driving home, she decided to hit the gym for an hour. She could then shower in ladies' locker room and use the change of clothing she kept in her locker for emergencies rather than drive home. She had not hit the gym in a few days since starting to hang out regularly with her new boyfriend Keith. As she went into the gym, she looked for the sign in sheet. You needed to sign in for insurance reasons and the department health kept an eye on this as physical fitness was a requirement of the job. It was also used to help keep the health insurance premiums down if officers exercise regularly. In addition, they could receive a bonus for lower health insurance premiums as part of the new union incentives.

Serena finally found the sheet under the table where it usually sits. Why it was there she had no idea. As she signed in, she looked at the names and timestamps.

Name	Time In	Time Out
Andy	5:30PM	7:45PM
David	6:15PM	7:15PM
Michael	7:30PM	8:15PM

Serena noticed that Jessica's name was not on the sheet. She had forgotten to sign the sheet in the past as well especially when she was in a rush. She signed the sheet and pulled out her cell phone. She looked for Jessica's department issued cell phone number and called. It rang a few times then went to voicemail. She did not leave a message. She sent a text to Andy asking *"Do you know what hospital Jessica is in?"* Serena was concerned for her coworker and somewhat friend. She was a single, pregnant woman with no family. Serena could relate to the no family part and wanted to see if she needed anything.

Serena got on the treadmill and put a

good 40 minutes in. At that point, she was a little tired from lack of sleep and a good workout combination. She took a shower and got dressed. She checked her phone. She had gotten a response from Andy while in the shower. *"Lenox Hill Hospital."* She closed the phone. She would call over there shortly. She pulled out her iPhone to check her e-mail. Mostly spam but one headline got her attention it was from the chief. **"Meeting at 7am!"** She clicked through to the message and read *"I need to see both of you in my office at 7am sharp about this investigation you are working on. Do not be late."* The "both of you" referred to her and Andy. She looked at the clock on her phone. She had about 30 minutes to eat and be in chief's office.

CHAPTER 9

Serena came out of the kitchen at the precinct with a cup of black coffee and a donut. A quick, not so healthy breakfast but good enough that she could function. She thought it was funny that the cop donut stereotype was true. She got the murder book together to get ready for her meeting. She flipped through and could tell Andy had done quite a bit of work on the book, helping them along to a finished product once the killer was caught.

She did a quick Google search for the number to Lenox Hill Hospital. She dialed the number it got picked up by a man after about 7 rings. "Lenox hospital. How can I help you?" "Hi, this is Detective Serena Triton, NYPD. I am calling because we have someone from our staff in your hospital and I would like to speak with her."

Serena knew with new Health Insurance Portability and Accountability Act (HIPAA) laws. They were not supposed to give out names of patients but saying you were a detective usually got you around that problem. The badge did not make the detective but made his or her job easier.

"What's the name?" Serena thought it worked. She gave him Jessica first and last name. "No, I am sorry no one by that name here." Serena was shocked. "Hmmm. She was just staying the night for observation. Maybe she was released early? Can you check that please?" "No, ma'am. I am sorry but no one by that name has been checked in or out in last 48 hours." "Thank You." She flipped the phone closed. She was confused. Where was Jessica and why would she lie about going to the hospital? A moment later, Andy showed up and knocked her out of her musings. "Serena, you ready for the chief?" "Yes I am ready. I have everything here."

They walk into the chief's office and Andy closed the door behind them. The chief was a middle aged man. He was getting in his last 2 years before he hit retirement age and could retired with a full police pension. He and his wife were recently looking at homes in the Pennsylvania mountains. Serena guessed after 20 years on the force he wanted the quiet life.

The chief Robert Riggs got right down to business. "What do we have on this case? Tell me some good news." Serena and Andy showed him the murder book along with all the evidence they had. They also shared their theories on the case. The chief looked impressed. He sat back in his chair. "You got all that in few days? You two work quickly. Here is the thing. I got the District Attorney's office breathing down my back to find this guy as soon as possible. It's one thing for a dirty cop to get killed or a defense attorney but when it's one of our own, we need to work harder." Serena knew the chief was not saying they were not working hard but the DA's office had a way of applying pressure especially with an election on the horizon.

The chief continued talking "You going to talk to Rice?" Andy chimed in. "Hopefully today, sir." "I want a report on my desk after you meet with Rice. We need to know what's going on. Anyone who touches this case ends up dead so watch your backs." he said with a tone of concern. Serena leaned back. "Sir, before we go, do you have an update on Jessica? Is she ok? Why was she not at work today?" "I got word from her. She is going to be out another day or so. Until then, we have a temp coming in to fill in for her. They keep cutting our budgets. They don't take cops off the street but they lay off lab people. Don't they realize how important they are to our operation?" the chief asks with a hint of bitterness. Andy chimes in again. "Chief, Jessica has been doing the job of two people since they laid the other lab tech off." "I know. I am in hopes to get us another lab person soon. Again watch your backs." He dismissed them.

As Andy opened the door and Serena walked out, she was concerned about where Jessica could be with this killer on the loose. She would like to talk to her and get confirm if she was ok.

"Andy I am going to the little girl's room for a minute. I will be back in second." Serena walked into the ladies' room. She always admired how clean it was. There were only 2 other women besides her in homicide so the bathrooms were pretty quiet and clean. This was quite unlike the men's bathroom that had more traffic than a train station as the girls on the force had come to say. She flipped open her cell phone and called Jessica's cell and it went right to voicemail. The only cell number she had was her work cell. Serena did not know her home phone or even if she had one or a personal cell. She could call Human Resources but by law they can't give it up. She then had an idea.

Jessica had a doctor's appointment the other day. Jessica and Serena shared the same OB GYN. She thought she might get lucky. She pulled out her iPhone and searched for the number and called. Someone answered after three rings "Hello, doctor's office." "Hi, my name is Detective Serena Triton of NYPD. I need to make an appointment for a checkup. My friend Jessica just reminded me the other day. She is having a baby and she was just there the other day." Serena hoped her hint would allow her to get some kind of clue.

"I am sorry. Are you sure you have the right office? I have no Jessica on my calendar for this past week." Serena is shocked. "What's going on with Jessica." She wondered to herself. She hoped that nothing is wrong with the baby and was concerned that Jessica was keeping secrets. "I have to run. I will call back." Serena flips the phone closed. Her worry for Jessica rose fast.

When Serena got back to her desk, she sat down. Andy could see the concern on her face. "You ok Serena?" Serena just shook it off. "I am fine. Just got stuff on my mind. When are we going to see Rice?" Andy got a grim look on his face and replied "The jail is waiting for us. Rice got shanked in the neck last night in his cell. He is dead and it's same killer. They left a pangram in blood on the wall." Serena's mouth opened wide. "How did he get inside to do the killing?" Andy stands up and grabs his suit jacket. "I don't know. Let's go check it out."

CHAPTER 10

Serena and Andy show up at the Metropolitan Correctional Center. They were required to show their IDs and give up their weapons. They were escorted in by the warden to show them the crime scene. As they approached the cell, Serena could smell blood. As she got to the cell, she saw the newest message written in blood.

"Sixty zippers were quickly picked from the woven jute bag RICE"

Serena walked into the cell and said, "This is different." Andy looks at Serena. "All the messages were different." Serena points out, making sure not to touch anything. "This time, the handwriting differs and the last name is all in capitals." Andy replies, "So you think this was someone on the inside being a copycat?" Serena replied "No, not a copycat.

This was a favor done on the inside." As Serena says that, Andy looks at the neck of victim. "There is a puncture wound here on the neck." He points and says, "The shaking was done afterwards. I bet if we get a toxicology report, DDT will be in his system." Serena looked at the warden. "Inmates don't have access to pesticides and such or syringes, correct?" The warden replies, "No ma'am. I mean, a syringe maybe, but not pesticides." Serena and Andy look at each other. "Any idea who did the shaking warden?" The warden replies "No, not yet, but I am going to be questioning my guards." Andy walks up to the warden. "Our forensics team will be here to take care of this soon. I am not sure who it will be because our current person's on maternity leave but here is my card. Once you question the guards, call me with whatever you have."

Serena and Andy started leaving the jail. Serena knew there were very few clues, if any; they were going to get from the jail cell. The truth was this was probably a favor done on the inside for someone, particularly the pangram killer. The question was how did the DDT pesticide get inside? That's what interested her the most.

Just as she got her gun back and reloaded it, she felt her phone buzz in her pocket. She looked it and saw it was a text from Keith. *"Hope all is well. I wish I could have spent more time with you. Going to class. Xoxo."* She felt bad she had taken off on Keith last night and never even gave him as much as a text. She replied back, *"Sorry about last night. Got hung up all day and have not slept yet."* She holstered her gun and gave back her visitor badge and headed out to car with Andy. Her phone buzzed again. *"No problem, I understand. Let me know when you're free."* Serena thought about how cute it was that he was being understanding and considerate.

As they got into the car, Andy looked over at Serena. "With Rice dead, we have a killer on the loose and no name to go on yet." Serena had a thought about the lawyer from last night that had be sedated. "What about the lawyer from last night?" Andy pulled out his phone to call the cop on duty at hospital. The officer answered after a few rings. Serena could not hear the conversation on the other end of the phone. All she could hear was Andy. "Ok, when the doctor gives the ok, let me know. You have my number. We need to speak to this guy ASAP." Andy put his phone away. "Doctor has not cleared him to talk to us yet. Maybe later today or tomorrow we will get a chance to speak with him first thing. A cop is staying on post till then."

Andy and Serena headed back to the station and stopped for lunch at a place they both really liked. They did not get to eat there often because they very rarely went to the jail on this side of town. They took a little longer then they should have to eat lunch as they were both running low on energy after working such long hours.

They got back to the precinct about hour before quitting time. Just as Serena sat down, the forensics technician who handled computers and cell phones came up to her desk. He had lots of acne, long hair down to his shoulders and looked to be in his very early twenties. "I was unable to pull anything off of the phone you gave me. It was wiped clean." Serena took the report and opened the manila envelope to read it. The tech stood there while she read the entire thing to herself. "This is just a long way of telling me data is unrecoverable until we get a subpoena and send it to Apple correct?" He replies, "Pretty much yeah. It takes a few weeks." Serena replies, "I understand that but we can't wait a few weeks. A killer is on the loose. As soon as you hear anything, or if you need anything from me to speed this up, let me know." The tech walked away and Serena looked at Andy. "I knew that was going to be an issue. We have had stuff like this happen before with tech."

Andy starts opening his mail. "Serena, here is the inventory from the ADA murder. There was a syringe with DDT in it found in drain under the Lexus. They were unable to pull a print, not even a partial. However, that does confirm your story that something happened and things did not go as planned."

Serena opens her cell phone and tries to call Jessica but gets the voicemail. She looks at Andy "Do you know Jessica's home address?" Andy replies "Why? What's up?" Serena replies back in a worried tone, "She has been gone for over two days. We have a killer on the loose. She's been close to the case and no one can get a hold of her. I want to drop by to make sure she is ok." Andy pulls out his iPhone. "I have her address here. My wife watered her plants once while she was away."

Andy rattles off the address to Serena. She writes it down in her notebook. "I am going to take a quick swing by just to make sure she is ok." Andy replies "It's on your time. No one will care. I just hope she does not get mad at me for giving you her home address." Serena looks up. "She will be fine with it. I will see you tomorrow." Serena grabs her coat and heads out to her car.

CHAPTER 11

Serena was surprised how fast she got downtown to Jessica's apartment. The parking garage was for residents only. She ended up having to park around the corner. She did not mind walking though and she headed to the main door by walking around the entire corner. When she got into the building, she pressed the elevator to go to the 3rd floor to Jessica's apartment. Once the door opens, she starts walking to the right looking for her apartment number 318. She found the apartment. The first thing she noticed was there was no mail on the floor like some of the other apartments which meant Jessica was home at some point today.

Serena knocked on the door. She waited and no one answered. Serena knocked harder and no one answered. She tried one last time, very hard, and the door opened.

Serena pushed the door open. "Hello! Jess? It's Serena!" She listened a moment and then called, "Jessica! It's Serena. The door was open."

Serena started walking around the apartment doing a room by room sweep. She was praying that she did not find Jessica tied up or, god forbid, killed. She started out in living room, then to the bedroom and bathroom. Jessica was nowhere to be found. As Serena headed to the door, she stopped for a moment to take in Jessica's book shelf. She was a big book reader and bookshelves always made her stop in her tracks despite the situation. She noticed titles like,

The Odyssey
Trojan Wars
Greek Gods
Vampire Diaries
True Blood

Serena noticed that most of the books were about Greek mythology and vampires. Serena knew that Jessica and she shared the same reading taste. Serena headed to the door and walked out into the hallway and pulled the door closed behind her. She saw what she assumed was a couple coming out of one of the other apartments. She walked over to the couple. She pulled her badge off her belt "Excuse me, Detective Serena Triton NYPD. Can you tell me how to get to the parking garage from here?" The coupled looked at her badge "Down the hall and to the left. Is everything ok with Jessica?" Serena quickly replied "Yes, she is just working a long case and she asked me to check in on her place." "So you to work together? That's cool. I hope Jessica is not over doing it. She is going to pop soon." Serena smiled and replied "Yes, I know. We have been telling her to take it easy." The couple smiled. "Tell her the neighbors were asking about her. Her spot number is 318 just like her apartment number."

Serena said thank you and headed down the hall and out into the parking garage. Serena walked the length of the parking garage on third level. Parking spot 318 was empty. She checked all the other spots on the third level and Jessica's car was nowhere to be found. She opened her cell phone and called dispatch. She asked if there were any cars like Jessica's reporting missing, abandoned or stolen. Dispatch told her no. She then realized Jessica was either staying with a friend or something was wrong. She tried her work number again and again voicemail.

Her cell vibrated. It was Keith. *"Hope all is well. I am home if you want to call and talk."* She was very close to Keith's house from where she was. Serena texted him back. *"I am only a few minutes from your house. Can I come over?"* He quickly texted back. *"Sure that would be great."*

She walked out the parking garage and headed around the block again to her car. The ride to Keith's house was short. One thing she noticed was there was metered parking all around Keith's apartment complex. She hung her police on duty tag to avoid getting a ticket since she had no change to use.

Serena had never been to Keith's apartment. Easy enough to find as the door buzzer had his name in big black letters by one of the buttons. She hit the buzzer. "Who is it?" Serena teases him. "NYPD! You're under arrest." Keith fires back in a laughing voice, "Maybe I should keep the door locked." Serena replies, laughing, "It's cold. Let me in you jerk." Serena walked up to Keith's apartment. He met her at the door with it open. She walked in and he offered to take her coat. Serena was hesitant as she liked to keep her gun concealed but Keith knew she had just come from work and had her department issued weapon.

Serena looked around Keith's apartment. It was much bigger than hers. His kitchen had much more counter space and was at the center of the apartment rather than hers in a tiny corner. Serena could tell the building was much more modern than hers. The bedroom had a very expensive sliding door and the room looked huge with a walk in closet and master bath. There was another bathroom by the kitchen and a second bedroom that had been turned into an office. All of Keith's furniture looked fairly new. The living room was fairly large with a table in the middle with, what looked like tests, Keith had been grading. Keith had a large flat screen TV on the wall with a surround sound system.

"This is a nice apartment you rent here." Serena says with a look of being impressed. "No I own it. It's a coop." Serena looks at Keith with a smile. "I guess I should let you buy dinner more often." Keith smiles as well. "No, it's not what you think. My grandmother left me some money when she died. I used it as down payment for this place." Those words echoed through Serena's head as she thought of the car dealership. She still had Jessica on her mind. She looked at the clock on Keith's wall. 6:00 PM, she was hungry and tired. She looked at Keith "Listen, I need get something to eat and..." Keith cut her off. "I already ate but I make great lasagna. It's fresh. I just made it today. Please stay and have some. Don't go out, you look tired." Keith rushed into the kitchen and pulled the lasagna tray from the fridge. He pulled the tin foil off then went into one of his upper cabinets to grab a plate then into one of the bottom draws to grab a spatula.

Serena was impressed how organized he was and how good the food looked. Keith then asked her, "Do you want me to put it in the oven?" Serena replied "Please, I am a detective. I am on call all the time and am used to the microwave." Keith covered the food with saran wrap and put it in microwave for three minutes. "Do you want wine with it? I have a great merlot." Serena said "No, I can't. I am on call so I am technically on duty. Do you have a soda?" Keith walks back and looks through his fridge. "I have one can of RC Cola left. Is that ok?" Serena smiled. "That's great. Perfect." "Do you want me to put it in a glass?" Serena smiled. "I am not fancy. I can drink it out of the can." Just as she said that, the microwave went off. Keith grabs a pot holder and pulls the food out of the microwave and places it in front of Serena. He opens the saran wrap.

Serena can smell the food as soon as he took the saran wrap off. It was obvious that Keith could cook much better than her. Keith opened the silverware drawer and handed her a fork. Serena took the food on the fork and blew on it to cool it as she took a mouth full. She looked at Keith. "Oh My God! This is amazing Keith." "Thank you. The secret is in my grandmother's sauce recipe."

Serena smiled. The two continued to talk while Serena was eating. Keith asked her questions about her day. Serena had to be careful what she said since certain things were still under investigation. She asked Keith about his day. He talked about his classes and students. She found him interesting. He always had something new to talk about.

After she was done eating, she remembered she had to give a report to the chief on Rice. She looked at Keith. "I am sorry but I have to make a call. I can clean up if you want when I am done." Keith smiled. "Don't worry about it. The dishwasher does the work." Serena flips open her phone and dials the chief's cell. She points to the empty room wanting privacy for the call. Keith nods his head and she walked into the second bedroom and closes the door.

The chief answers. "Triton! What took you so long to call?" She replied back, "Hello Chief. You said end of day and I was still working up until about half hour ago." She knew this was a bit of a fib but wanted to make the chief happy. "I talked to your partner Andy. He told me about Rice. I mean Jesus Christ; we need to get this under control! People are getting kill even in lockup now. I got a 24/7 guard by that other attorney. He is our only lead now if he saw anything at all." Serena said "He is a long shot." Chief says, "I know that Triton but we got nothing else. Andy got a call from the doctor. They sedated him. You can talk to him tomorrow." Serena replied, "Tomorrow morning first thing it is chief." "Triton listen, this guy is still on the loose. Watch your back. No one is safe." "I always have one in the chamber chief." She flipped the phone closed and leaned against the door. Having one in the chamber was an old cop term for being ready to shoot. She was still worried about Jessica but did not want to tell anyone yet. If she did not hear from her tomorrow, she was going to alert the chief.

She flipped her phone open and called Jessica's cell again. It went to voicemail. When she heard the beep, she left a message. "Jessica, it's Serena. I am not trying to bother you. I hope you and baby are ok. Listen, we got that killer on the loose and he is going after anyone close to the case. Please check in with me. We all just want make sure you're ok. Thanks and call me back anytime." Serena flipped the phone closed.

She walked out of the room. Keith was sitting on the couch. She sat next to him and put her head on his shoulder. She was exhausted. She felt her eyes get heavy and she yawned. Just then, she felt herself safe and drifting off to sleep.

CHAPTER 12

Serena jumped as she realized she had fallen asleep. She quickly looked at the clock and saw it was 6 AM. She sighed in relief, she was still early. She sat up and realized that Keith was already up cooking breakfast. She looked around. She was on Keith's couch and had a blanket over her. She noticed her gun was still on her hip along with her badge.

Keith had a huge smile on his face as she turned to look at him. "I hope you like eggs." Serena was not a morning person. It was apparent Keith was as she rubbed her eyes. "Eggs are fine. Do you have coffee?" Keith replies, very chipper, "Yep, light and sweet like you like it." Serena smiled. He had remembered from the coffee shop the other night. She was impressed with a man that listened to her needs. "Sorry I slept on your couch." "It's no big deal. I let you sleep. I went into my room and retired early myself." Serena pulled her hair back in a ponytail. She had no time for a shower and no time to go home and get new clothes. She remembered she had also used her extra clothing in her locker from the all nighter she had pulled.

"I don't suppose you have a spare toothbrush?" Serena asked while tying up her hair and fixing her blouse. "Actually I do in the bathroom. It's on the top shelf there, brand new." Serena, with look of curiosity, wondered "How many girls sleep over here?" Keith smiled. "Not girls, just drunken friends." "I am sure that's what you tell all the girls." Serena smirked and stuck her tongue out at him.

She brushed her teeth and washed up a bit with the towel and washcloth that was on one of the shelves. Her phone vibrated and she saw it was Andy. "*Meet me at hospital. ETA?*" Serena thought about where hospital was in relation to where she was and traffic conditions. She texted back. "*About 40 minutes.*" Serena came out of bathroom and said, "I am sorry I have to go. My partner called." "No big deal. I packed you breakfast in this paper bag and a travel mug of coffee." She took the bag and cup kissed him on the cheek and rushed to her car. She put her light on the top of her car and stepped on it. She ate her egg sandwich in between lights and drank a few sips of coffee.

She got to the hospital and noticed several police cars. "This was not good." She thought to herself. There was only supposed to be one cop on duty at time. She parked her car and left light on so she did not get a ticket Andy was in the lobby of the hospital along with the chief and another uniformed officer. Serena walks in the front door of the hospital and asked "What happened?" Andy replies "Someone got to our lawyer last night." Serena was shocked. "What? How? He was under surveillance." The chief says with a loud, annoyed voice, "Officer Smith here went for a bathroom break and the perp must have been waiting for the right moment and that was it. He is going to be doing months of parking enforcement make up for it."

Serena then asks "Are we sure it's the pangram killer?" Andy pulls an evidence bag out of his pocket with a doctor's script page with a pangram that reads,

*"The public was amazed to view the
quickness and dexterity of the juggler."*

After reading, Serena noted that the
pangram was a bit of a dig on them for not
being able to protect their witness. Serena then
says, "There has to be security footage." Andy
replies, "They're pulling the footage now.
Should only be a few minutes." The chief gets
more upset as he comes into the conversation.
"We got nothing to go on. Every damn witness
is dead and anyone that gets close to the case
is dead. We got find this guy! Everyday there is
another murder. This footage better be
something."

Out of the elevator comes a man with
frosted blond hair, green eyes and very pale
skin. "Officers, my apologies for the wait. My
name if Guy. We wanted to make sure we
have the footage you need. We have video of
your killer. Follow me please." The man had a
British accent and Serena thought that fact of
his name being Guy was funny. They walk into
a room around the corner from where they
were standing. As Serena walked in, she
noticed about 20 computer monitors all with
different views of the hospital. Guy points to
the screen to the far left and tells the guard to

play the file on the desktop. "Yes right there. Yes, click that one marked police_today." The gentleman double clicked the video and the file opened and started to play. The video showed the officer sitting on the chair and, after about minute of video, the officer got up and left. Not even a minute later, a person in black trench coat and mask walked into the room and was out not even a minute later.

Serena then said, "Where is the footage from the other cameras? Are there parking lot cameras?" Guy replies, "We have no parking lot cameras and that section of the hospital is old. The cameras are sparse and don't work that well. We're hoping to get them replaced next year in the renovation." The chief says in a nasty tone, "Well that does not help us! Now this person has killed five people and that's all you have." Serena asked, "Can we have a copy of the footage?" Guy pulls a jump drive out of his pocket. "I have it right here officers. I am sorry I can't do more for you." Serena took the jump drive and put it in her pocket. They watched the video a few more times and start walk out of the room.

The chief then asks, "This footage is almost useless. Do we need any special software to play that video?" Guy replied "No, absolutely not. We upgraded the server last year. All the video files we pull can be opened in Quicktime or Windows media player. We went top of the line." The chief replies, getting more annoyed, "Maybe next time spend money on cameras first." Guy replies quickly and with an annoyed tone, "Listen sir, we are a public hospital. Everything comes down to budget. It's hard to justify better security when we need to spend money to buy dialysis machines to save lives. I am sure you face the same issues in some form with your department." The chief sighs and extends his hand in gesture of apology. "Fair enough argument Guy. Thank you for your help in any case." Serena could tell that the chief and Guy both understood each other's issues. Any state run organizations have to weigh wants versus needs when it came to finances.

Serena starts talking to Andy. "How did this happen? Judging by the video, this happened around 5 PM. This just found the body this morning." Andy replies, "By time blood work and autopsy came back from the morgue, not to mention the time it took to call 911and then find out whose case it was, you can only imagine the confusion. We're lucky it got to us this fast." Serena replies, "I am going to wait for them to check the room then I will meet you at the station." Andy replies, "Good idea. If they find anything, call me." Serena, taking a page out of the chief's book says, "Watch your back partner."

CHAPTER 13

Serena got back to the station late. She was upset it took so long to process the crime scene. The hospital chief of staff was concerned about hospital liability and patient care so they had to wait until all the patients got moved to different wing of the hospital. The hospital then had to check with their lawyers to make sure they were allowed to let the NYPD forensic team check the room and examine the body.

Serena walked in the squad room and sat at her desk. Andy asked, "What took you so long?" Serena replied annoyed, "Took hours. Bureaucracy at its finest." Serena explained the entire story to Andy. "I guess you will think twice before volunteering to stay and watch the crime scene." Serena rolled her eyes then smiled. "You got that right." Serena pulled the jump drive out of her pocket and plugged it into the computer. She copied the video to her local C: drive then unplugged the jump drive. "I am going to take this over to tech forensics. Maybe they can do something with this."

Serena walks over to the tech forensics employee, which she still could not remember his name. "Excuse me, can you look at this video file and see if you can enhance it?" The kid looked up at her. "That's easy. Should take an hour, maybe less." Serena smiled at him. "Can it be done today? The pangram killer is still on the loose." He looks back. "Yeah, I will drop it on your desk before I leave today." "Thank You." Serena hands him the drive. She walked back to her desk and saw Jessica. She was going over information about hospital forensics with Andy. Serena felt a feeling of relief in her stomach.

Serena yelled out, "Glad your back! Did you get my message yesterday?" Jessica replied, "I did. Thank you so much for your concern but I was down for the count at my place for last few days. I really overdid it working out. I am staying away from the downstairs gym until after my pregnancy is over. That's when I'll need to get my body back." Serena made sure to show no expression in her face. "Take care of you and that baby first. Worry about your body shape later." Jessica smiled and joked, "I have one shape right now, round." She giggled. Andy thanked her for the report and Jessica headed back to her lab. Serena sat there and wondered why Jessica would be trying to keep a secret. Was she having health issues, legal issues or problem with her baby's father? She looked at the clock. It was later in the day and she still had work to do before she left. She had to update the murder book and she had to inventory evidence.

Serena spent next few hours doing her paperwork. It was a daunting task but it had to be done. She looked at the clock again. It was getting close to end of day. She leaned back in her chair. She was about to flip open her phone and call Keith when she saw an email come in on her computer. It was titled,

Your Video You Needed Today

Serena wondered why the case number was not included in the email but then disregarded it. She opened the email. It was the enhanced image of the hospital video. She noticed the email was from techforensics@precinct.54.gov. That ruled out the idea of at least finding out the tech's username so she could thank him by name. She opened the video and started watching it. The quality was a little better but not much. She watched it several times forward and backward and she could not make out a face.

She slammed back in her chair. "Damn It!" Andy looks over with a concerned look. "What's wrong?" Serena exhaled in frustration and said, "I still can't make out the damn face of our killer." Andy replied, "OK, give me a minute I will take a look at it shortly." Serena gets another email titled,

Phone Logs

She was going to open it when she heard Andy say, "Whoever the killer is, he is not in the greatest of shape. I think we can rule out the gym as a place to find him. He looks like he has a beer belly by the black sweatshirt he is wearing." Serena got up and looked at video again. The killer was about 5 feet and 10 inches and close to 250 pounds. "It had to be a man.", she thought to herself.

Andy looked at his watch. "Serena, I got

to go. Tomorrow we can see what the chief wants to do with the trail as it's pretty cold. The feds will probably be brought in to look at things. They have profilers and access to some resources we don't." Serena was annoyed. All the work they had done and now the FBI was going to come in and take the credit after her and Andy and her team did most of the heavy lifting. Andy put his jacket on and left, telling Serena he would see her tomorrow.

She sat back at her desk and flipped her phone open to text Keith. "*I have had a hell of a day. How are you?*" Serena flipped her phone closed. The forensic tech walked by her desk. "Did you get my email? I was able to get a log file off that phone. I never knew you could do that. A friend of mine from the 50th precinct told me what to do. It's only the last few calls from the recent call log. Apparently Apple has a security flaw and has a patch coming out, but for right now this security hole has been helping us in tech."

Serena smiled and said, "No, I did not receive your email. I will take a look. Thank you." Serena opened her email and saw one from David.Romen@precinct.54.gov. "Well, mystery solved." she thought to herself. She could call him Dave now when she saw him. She downloaded the log file and to her surprise, opened in notepad rather than word. She would ask the newly named Dave about that later. There were three numbers on the log and she was disappointed as that was all she was going to get. She could request the numbers to be broken to find out who they belonged to, but that would take time. Just then, her phone buzzed and she saw it was Keith. She flipped the phone open to see, "*Sorry to hear. I hope to see you soon. Let me know when you're free.*"

She sat there looking at the three numbers. One caught her eye with the 631-555 exchange. A few years ago, to standardize the NYPD, the department bought the entire block on the 631-555 exchange. No one else but NYPD had that. It was a huge purchase for NYPD but it made things easier. Plus, the phone company was happy because they got back a lot of old numbers they wanted to decommission. Serena knew this because Andy had told her a story about how easy his number was and he was forced to give it up for the number he had now.

She pulled up the NYPD phone

directory. Only NYPD had access to it, not that it was anything special. It was just an excel spreadsheet with everyone's name and number and what type of phone they had. As she scrolled through the names, she noticed several people that started after her that were issued new iPhones. She would bring this up with her captain when he returned from his two week vacation he was on. That's why they were dealing with the chief of police because he was covering for her boss along with the severity of the case.

When she found the number, she was shocked. The last number Zuriel called before his death was Jessica and she remembered Gabriel, the waitress she had interviewed, said she found his body around 7:30 AM. The cell phone call was time stamped in the logs around 7:00 AM. If Zuriel had talked to Jessica thirty minutes before his death, why had Jessica not mentioned that? That would have been useful information. Serena looked at the video again from the hospital. She was confused now. She pulled the Rice case from her desk and went to the surviving cop's testimony. He describes one of the attackers as being 5 feet and 8 inches tall with a ponytail. Neither Rice nor Zuriel had long hair. She sat back to think.

She kept watching the video from hospital over and over. Something caught her eye. The killer had a pair of high heel boots about 2 inch heels high from what she could tell. Serena then thought the killer was not 5' 10". The woman was 5' 8" and had 2 inch heels on. It was a clever trick. The attacker was not a man but a woman. She continued to watch the video when it hit her like a bolt of lightning. The woman did not have a beer belly, she was pregnant.

She then looked at the time stamp on the video. It was 5:38. She had gotten to Keith's around 6 and his place was 10 minutes away from Jessica's apartment. She was not home and her car was not in the parking garage. Jessica had a long ponytail. She was trained in how to use a weapon. It all fit and she had books on her shelf about Greek mythology. Serena knew at that point Jessica was the third person involved in the heist. She was the pangram killer.

CHAPTER 14

Serena sat in her desk chair blown away. One of their own was the killer and had been right under her nose. All the time she spent worried that Jessica she was hurt, she was sympathizing with her. She was never in any danger; she was the killer. Serena knew she could not just walk into the chief's office with this. She would have to confront Jessica first. She looked at the clock and saw it was after 6 PM. Jessica was gone, probably on her way home. Serena knew she had to confront her and get the truth. Serena grabbed her jacket and headed to her car. She thought about calling Andy but she was afraid. What if she was wrong? She would have a black mark against her for suspecting a fellow officer. She could not risk that in her new job.

Serena felt like it took forever to get to Jessica's apartment. No red light, no siren; she did not want to arouse suspicion. As she walked up to Jessica's, she thought about pulling her gun but dismissed it as a bad idea. She did not want to escalate the confrontation if she didn't have to. She stood at the third floor entrance, pondering about what to say. She noticed some junk mail papers in the garbage can next to her. One was a large empty USPS priority mail envelope. She picked it up and put a few papers into it. That was going to be her cover story to get in the apartment without the use of force.

She put the envelope under her arm and walked to 318 and knocked. She heard Jessica's voice call out, "Hello!" "Jessica, it's Serena. I have an envelope of evidence I need you to look at. Andy gave me your home address. It's really important. I know you're off work now but it's important, please." Jessica yelled through the door, "Ok! One Second!" As the door opened, Serena walked through and immediately felt something slam into back of her head.

The next thing Serena knew was she was waking up with her handcuffs on her wrists in front of her. She quickly went to reach for her gun and found it was missing. She had a headache and was a bit light headed. She figured she had a concussion from whatever slammed her on the head. Jessica was sitting on a chair a few feet from Serena with her gun aimed at her. She was wearing a red dress and the same spiked boots she was wearing in the hospital video. Serena, still groggy, asked softly "How did you know that I knew?" "Wasn't hard. I got wind of the phone records Dave gave you and my neighbors told me you were here last night. I knew you would figure it out. You're smart girl." Serena's head was pounding. "Zuriel… You and Rice pulled the heist. Am I right?" "Yes, that's correct." was the reply. "Why did you kill Zuriel?" Jessica replied, "He was going to send up a red flag by buying that stupid sports car. What did he think? He could drive that to work and no one would know?" That actually made sense to Serena. How was he going to drive that and not raise suspicion? "What did you kill Davis for? Was it because Rice confessed to him? Lawyer client privilege not enough for you?"

"Davis knew the truth. He was cutting a deal with Rice to give me and Zuriel up." Serena's head was now reduced to a dull ache. She replied, with her voice getting stronger, "That does not explain the bruises on his neck. You killed him with DDT." "I had nothing to do with the bruising. He was just into some kinky stuff with his girlfriend. I am innocent of that." "Then how did you kill him in the pool?" Jessica's tone became flat. "I killed him first then threw him in pool to wipe away the evidence." "How about the ADA? Why was he brutally killed?"

Jessica pondered a minute. "That was not my fault. I broke the window then went to give him the shot of DDT. He opened the car door and hit my stomach. I started having cramps and dropped the syringe. I had no choice but to beat him over the head. I would have preferred a cleaner kill. I did overdue my exercise just not on the department issued treadmill." Serena knew that was the case. The ADA murder just felt sloppy. "And the witness could have made you, that's why you killed him in hospital." Jessica smiles at her handy work. "That's correct." "Answer me this? How did you kill Rice on inside?"

Jessica starts rubbing her belly. "Wow, this kid's kicking." Serena noticed Jessica's breathing became heavy. "My boyfriend is an inmate there. I have conjugal visits with him. That's how I got pregnant 8 months ago. He was supposed to be our fourth man; however he got picked up on a drug charge about 2 weeks before we did the heist. He owed me. Not only because I'm the mother of his child but he also screwed up the job. If we would have had him, no one would have been killed."

Serena then asked, "Why the pangrams?" Jessica replied, "The truth is I like Greek mythology. Rice knew that. I knew he had access to the news. I was hoping he would get the point but I guess not. After I killed Davis, he told same story to the ADA." Serena put something else together in her head. "Since you're the head of a forensics team, you have access to warehouse records. That's how you knew the money was there." Jessica smiled smugly and said, "You got it. That money sitting there would have been used to fund campaigns and buy office furniture. Stupid shit for overpaid government workers. They say it goes back in the police department. If that's true, why do they keep laying off forensics workers? We are the ones in the labs making the detectives, captains, lieutenants and commissioner look good. It was time we took our bonus." Serena shifted a bit and said "You knew Zuriel had SWAT training and access to weapons because he worked the cage at our station. That's how you knew he would be a good person to work with. But what about Rice?" "He was just my boyfriend's friend who we brought in to help. He had some military training and why not? We needed the manpower."

Jessica suddenly clutched her stomach in pain. Serena knew something was wrong. "Jessica listen, have you been having pains for the last few days? If so, you need medical attention." Jessica pointed the gun at her. "I am not going to jail." Serena urgently said, "Jessica I care about the baby. Let me help you." Jessica pointed the gun more solidly and replied "No."

Jessica got rocked by another hard contraction. Serena thrust back on the chair she is sitting on and the chair flies backward. Jessica cried out and went over the chair. Serena made an attempt to grab her but Jessica smacked Serena hard across the face. As Jessica got up, she held her stomach and screamed in pain. "Serena, back off! I don't want shoot you!" Serena moved in closer. Jessica aimed at a wall mounted lamp and pulled the trigger. The bullet hit the lamp and glass shattered all in Serena's face. She felt the pain as glass cut the skin of her face and landed in her eyes.

Serena hit the ground and rolled behind the counter. She heard a door open and close. She assumed it was Jessica fleeing the scene. She was able to open her left eye as it was the one farthest from the point of impact from the glass. She reached in her right sock and pulled out her extra handcuff key. She uncuffed herself and got up. She saw her phone on the table next to the couch where she was sitting. She flipped it open to find a text from Keith that read *"Miss you tonight. Xoxo."* She had hard time reading what it said but she got general idea. She thought to herself, "You have no idea how much I miss you today, Keith."

She hit speed dial for Andy. It rang twice before he answered. "Serena, what's up?" She said hurriedly, "I am at Jessica's apartment. I need backup and bring paramedics." Andy replied, "I am on my way." Serena hung up and stumbled into the bathroom and locked the door. She braced herself against it and knew she was very vulnerable without her sight. She hoped would be safe until Andy got there to help her.

CHAPTER 15

The sun was setting as Serena sat on a gurney in an ambulance. She told Andy the entire story as the paramedic pulled the pieces of glass out of her face and around her eyes. The paramedic says to Serena, "You're lucky Detective. If you did not turn your head and close your eyes, this glass would have done much more damage." Serena was happy to hear that the damage to her eyes was not as severe as she thought. The medic pulled another piece and she winced, exclaiming "Owww! That hurts!" "I am sorry Detective. Some of these are very deep. Please sit as still as you can. We really should bring you into the hospital for stitches." Serena snapped, "No, I am not going to the hospital. You can stitch me up later."

Andy was leaning against the ambulance. Serena can see him out of the corner of her eye. "You're lucky she missed, partner." he said. Serena replied as the medic removed more glass, "She was not aiming... Ouch! at me Andy. If she wanted me dead, she would shot center mass. She had a clear shot and Jessica knows how to use a firearm. She said "Stay back. I don't want to shoot you." The paramedic interrupts her by saying, "Please hold this." He puts gauze on the wound where the glass was just removed. "That really needs a stitch." Serena winces then says sarcastically, "Lucky for me, I clot fast." The medic shook his head and sighed. He said, resigned, "You're all done detective. Just give me a second to get some paperwork for you to sign."

She turned to look at Andy. "Do you know where she would go?" Andy replied, "She does not have any family so I am not sure where she would go to hide." "Andy, she is labor from what I can tell. She needs safe place to have the baby. She won't check into a hospital, not with an APB out on her. Not to mention we have patrolmen faxing over pictures of her to all local clinics and urgent care centers. She can't leave country either since we alerted homeland security." Just as she finished, the paramedic came up to her with a clipboard. "Ok detective, what this says is you are refusing to let me take you to the hospital for additional medical care. This relieves me of any and all responsibility. You are refusing care against medical orders." Serena looked at him with a look of disgust. By this point, her head had stopped bleeding so she threw the gauze in the ambulance trash. "Thanks for all your help. I will make sure check with my eye doctor." She scribbled her signature on the paperwork.

She knew the paramedic was just doing his job but she had a job to do as well. Find a killer on the loose. She walked around the front of the ambulance then down the alley where she saw her car. Andy followed. As they approached the car, Serena took out her keys and popped the trunk. Andy asked "What are you doing?" She looked back and said "I have blood all over me. I just remembered that I have a spare shirt in the trunk. Can you turn around please?" He turned his back to Serena. Even though they were close partners, Serena still had a few things she was not ready to show Andy. She unbuttoned her blouse and threw it in the trunk and then pulled out a black V neck t-shirt out of a bag. She pulled it over her head and said "Ok Andy. You're good. You can look now." He turned back around and she asked "Do you have my gun?" Andy replied "No, it was nowhere to be found. It's not even on the evidence list from the apartment."

Serena was shuffling around in the trunk of her car. "Crap that means Jessica has it and according to my calculations, she has 14 shots left." Serena pulled another gun out from the bag she had her t-shirt in. Andy asked "Is that your backup?" Serena replied "Yes. I took it the range other day. Do you have an extra mag?" Andy reached around to the back of his belt and pulled out a spare clip and handed it to Serena. They both understood no cop wanted to walk around unarmed while in pursuit of an armed suspect. She forced the clip into the gun and chambered a round but left the safety on. She looked at Andy in relief and said "Thanks. I knew you would understand."

They both got into the Mustang with Serena driving. They sat there and brain stormed for a minute. Serena then put her head up. "She said that she had conjugal visits with her boyfriend but working for the police department, she would never give her real name." Andy replied back, thoughtfully "Well, conjugal only happens once every few weeks at that prison. They have a mobile trailer with a few rooms and whoever's turn it is for conjugal gets one of those rooms. We could go through the names of the last few months." Serena had an idea and with an excited tone said,"No, wait! Pulling records from the last few months will be a shot in the dark. Jessica is 8 months pregnant! Pull records from 8 months ago and we should be able to narrow it down. If we cross reference it with the inmates and what they got arrested for, we should be able to find her."

Andy pulled out his phone. "Let me look for the Warden's information in my iPhone." Serena starts the car and starts heading in the direction of the station. "Have him email or fax over the records." She then smiled and said "By the way, you're a friend of the captain's. You need to work on getting me a better phone then this flip phone. There are some people who have been here for less time and have a smartphone." Andy looked over and shook his head and chuckled at her as he put the phone to his ear. "I will work on that."

They arrived at the station and as they walked in the door, the chief stopped them. "Tell me good news you two. I got the commissioner calling me asking how we did not know one of our own was the killer." Andy replied quickly, "We have a solid lead chief and we're working on it." The chief nodded and replied "Good keep me in the loop." He hurried away to answer an insistently ringing phone.

"Serena, I am going to get those records off the fax machine. I will be back." Serena thanked Andy. She headed to their office and sat down at her computer and logged in. Andy was back momentarily with the paperwork. He handed her a copy of paperwork and said "Someone was nice enough to make copies for us." Serena smiled and looked at her desk calendar for the date to look for or around that date. Serena gazed over the copy and then yelled "Andy! We're in luck! Only one conjugal truck was at the prison for the month we need." Andy looked up from his copy and replied "I see that. So there are 4 women we need to check out." He started flipping through paper work. "Look at page 7."

She found the page and four women along with who they were visiting were listed. "Andy, Jessica said her boyfriend was arrested for drug charges. Pull the rap sheet on them and that will help narrow it down." He typed away at the keyboard. "That narrows it down. We have two people now."

Serena puts her hand on her chin and thought about her conversation with Jessica just hours ago. She remembered a key piece of evidence. "Look at when they were arrested. Jessica said he was arrested two weeks before the heist. Check that date." Andy looked up at Serena. "One woman under the name of Terry Shaw." Serena continued to bark orders. "Call the Warden again and have him fax over the copy of the ID they have on file. They have to have copy of the driver's license or state issued ID to allow her into the prison. We can confirm from that." Andy opened his phone and called the warden. He was on phone with him when her phone vibrated. It was Keith calling. She had not spoken to him all day. She needed to take this. She flipped the phone open.

"Keith, we have an emergency at the station. Can I call you later?" Keith said "Sure but can you just tell me if you're ok and safe?" She replied back "Yes, I am safe and fine. I will call you later." Keith said "OK, love you." and hung up. Serena sat shocked. Had she just heard that correctly? She was about to call him back when Andy slammed the paper on her desk and said triumphantly, "There she is wig and all." Serena looked and the one thing she noticed was Jessica had been wearing a bad wig. She could not see the color of the hair because the fax was black and white but she was sure it was a wig.

Andy smiled. "I have couple of officers putting homeland security and hospitals on alert for Terry Shaw. I got a copy of Jessica's bank records and I have them monitoring for any activity. If we get any hits, they will call us. We have her boxed in. It's just waiting game now." Serena didn't think Jessica would use her bank account when she was being hunted. She would not be that stupid. She was smart and she knew police procedure.

She was jolted from her thoughts when Andy said "Listen Serena, it's late. I got to get out here. My wife needs me go home. When we get a hit on something, they will call." She nodded and said "I will head out in a bit. See you tomorrow Andy." She watched him grab his jacket and leave. Serena knew that Andy had family and had spent a lot time on this case. He had other obligations besides work.

She sat there looking through Jessica's bank statement. "Bills and more bills just like all of us." she thought. She decided to look through the records one at a time and break down each one.

Con Edison NY - the electric bill for her apartment
NYC WaterWorks - her water bill
AT & T - Her phone or internet
Macy's - Probably a credit card
Grange Insurance - probably car insurance
PA Department Of Property Tax - *Serena would go back to this one*
Time Warner Cable - TV Service
Amazon Corp - Probably a credit card

Serena went through the entire list of charges for last month and the only one that stuck out to her was the **PA Department Of Property** Tax. Why would Jessica send them a check? Serena looked at the time. It was heading for 11 PM so she figured she would get the number and try calling. She Googled the number and called.

After a few rings, the phone was picked up. Serena thought "What luck." She quickly spoke to not lose the person on the phone. She might not get a second chance. "Hi. This is Serena Triton from the NYPD. I am working a case and this number was given to me. I am sorry it's so late. I would not have called if it was not an emergency." The lady responded. She sounded elderly but Serena did not care. She was happy to get someone on the phone this late at night. "We have our yearly tax sale tomorrow. I am here getting ready for it. Normally I would be home watching my stories." Serena thought to herself "I would rather be home with my new boyfriend who just told me he loves me." She hummed an agreeable sound and said "I am sorry to hear that. Listen, I will only take 5 minutes of your time. Do you have any property under this name?" She gave Jessica's first and last name to the lady and she replied "No, I am sorry sweetheart but I have no one by that name." Serena said "Try Terry Shaw." The lady immediately came back with "Oh yes. I remember talking to that girl several times on the phone. She has a cabin up here in the mountains and she wanted to send me cash. Said she had to pay 3 years of back property taxes but I told her it had to be a personal check or money order."

Serena thought that was it Jessica's one misstep. If she had sent a money order rather than a personal check, Serena would have had no way to find out she had a property under a different name in another state. Serena then quickly focused and asked "Can you please give me the address?" The older women gave her the address and Serena thanked her and hung up the phone. She had never heard of a place call Damascus in the Pocono Mountains. She typed in the address "118 Deer Graze Road Damascus, PA" into Google maps." From what she could tell, it was mostly farmland and would be a four hour ride from the city. "Well, I'm wide awake. Might as well check it out." She thought to herself. There was no guarantee Jessica would be there but it wouldn't hurt to look.

CHAPTER 16

Before Serena left, she went downstairs
to get a shower in the women's locker room in
the precinct gym. When she was done and in
her car, she punched the address into the
dashboard GPS. She swung through a drive
thru for a large coffee and breakfast sandwich
and stopped at gas station for a fill. She
looked down at the GPS and saw the time read
4 hours and 11 minutes. It was almost 2am by
this point. She would be there by 6am or later.
She could not call Keith as he was in bed by
this point and so was Andy. She just wanted to
see what the deal with this cabin was. The
odds of Jessica making it 4 hours away in labor
were slim but it was all she had to go on at this
point. Plus, she was not kind of detective to
leave something like this alone.

As the hours rolled by, she noticed the
gorgeous countryside. If she was ever going to

have a baby, she would want it to be out here in the country not in the busy city. It was more peaceful and laid back. She did not see any signs of crime or police. "A perfect place for a hideouts." she thought.

The ride went by quick. She noticed the GPS said the destination would be on her right. She pulled off on the side of the road about 1000 yards from the house. She noticed a Jeep with PA plates. It was a small log cabin in the middle of nowhere. She slowly walked to the house and pulled out her gun. She approached the Jeep and felt the hood. It was cold and that meant that whoever was inside had not been out for a ride.

She walked up the stairs slowly so not to be heard. She stayed close to the wall and peeked into the window on the front door. Her eyes widened in shock as she saw Jessica. She was lying on the floor propped up with a few pillows behind her covered in a blanket with blood on it holding a newborn baby. Serena opened the door slowly. She knew Jessica still had her gun somewhere. She walked in and Jessica looked at her. She had tears in her eyes. "He is precious isn't he?" Jessica asked in tears to Serena. Serena was still standing with her gun pointed. Jessica sniffed and said "You don't have to be afraid. Your gun is right up there on the table." Serena walked over to the kitchen table and grabbed the gun and unloaded it.

She turned and said "You know I have to take you in." Jessica smiled while still crying. "I know and I knew you would find me I just wanted to give birth to him and hold him. I am sorry you got hit in face with glass. I was just trying to get away. I was never going to kill you." Serena nodded as she understood. Jessica said "I just want to hold him for a little longer. I know once they come, they will take him from me and I will never see him again." She paused, cuddling her baby boy. "The money is in that bag. Most of it anyway. I used about 10 grand but that's it." Serena nodded again.

"Serena, I never wanted to kill anyone. After I got pregnant, all I could think about was this little guy. If I could have gone back, I would have never done the heist. He is more important than any money in the world. I killed those people in hopes that the trail would go cold and I could have my baby in peace. I had hoped the case would go into archives forever.

I just wanted to be a mother." Serena squatted down next to her and looked at Jessica's new son. He was only maybe an hour old and would never know his mother. He would grow up in foster care, a product of the system, no parents to guide him. Serena's eyes suddenly welled in tears. She missed her dad.

Jessica looked at her. "How long until they get here?" Serena replied back "No one is coming. No one knows I am here or that I found you." She paused to collect herself and then asked "You had the Jeep hidden under a different name with PA plates. That's how you got out here?" Jessica nodded.

Serena gazed at the two for a long moment. She then stood up and walked toward the door. She paused and turned around. "As far as I am concerned, I never found you but that does not mean someone else won't. You're a wanted woman with 3 million in cash and a new baby. I won't tell anyone I found you but I am not going to protect you either." Jessica nodded. "Thank you Serena. You have my word you will never hear from me again. Not personally or in the news, I am done. I am just a mom now, nothing more."

Serena holstered her gun and walked out. She heard Jessica's voice through the door when she closed it. "You're the best damn detective in that whole precinct. Not because you let me go but because you care. Don't let the job take over. Find a man you love and have babies. There is nothing better than being a mom Serena. Kids change your life for the better. I know, I am example of that." Serena walked down the stairs and headed to her car. She hit the directions for home and would make sure to destroy the GPS later so no one ever found Jessica.

After about an hour on road, her phone rang. She picked it up and Keith jumped into conversation. "I never heard from you last night. I hope all is well." Serena had smile on her face. "All is well. How about dinner at my place tonight? It's my turn to cook." Keith sounded happy. "Sounds great." Serena had a feeling in pit of her stomach. She had to say it. "Keith, I have to go. I will see you tonight. Love you." She flipped the phone closed.

Epilogue

Serena was happy to see that the news had forgotten about the Pangram Killer headline and moved on to other hot stories. Andy looked over Jessica's bank statement that Serena had looked over and but found no connection. When Serena asked the chief if they were going to bring in the FBI, he said they were too busy with terrorist threats.

Serena knew the case was going head down into archives since the trail went cold. Over time, it would be picked up by the open unsolved unit. Serena did not care. She put all the paperwork she had in the file. If no one else put it together, Jessica was free, but Serena was not going to protect her either. If open unsolved got a lead or put it together like she did, Jessica was on her own.

Serena was not worried about Jessica anymore. She had other interests now. She looked at the 8 x 10 picture Keith had blown up for her on her wall. It was of the two of them in the woods. It was a weekend trip they had taken to a place in the Poconos. She smiled as she remembered Jessica's advice. She found a man she loved and would hopefully marry him and have his children.

ABOUT THE AUTHOR

It's been a life goal of mine to write and book and now I have officially accomplished that goal. I have worked on many blogs and written many short stories but to me writing a book was something I have always want to do because of my love for reading. Please contact me on my website http://brandonlipani.com to discuss my book or book signing appearances.

If you are a library or book club and are interested in my book please contact me at the website listed.

There will be more Serena Triton novels to come in the future please keep on the lookout for them.

Made in the USA
Charleston, SC
31 December 2015